BBC
DOCTOR WHO

THE
DANGEROUS
BOOK OF
MONSTERS

BBC CHILDREN'S BOOKS
UK | USA | Canada | Ireland | Australia
India | New Zealand | South Africa

BBC Children's Books are published by Puffin Books,
part of the Penguin Random House group of companies
whose addresses can be found at global.penguinrandomhouse.com.
puffinbooks.com

Penguin
Random House
UK

First published by Puffin Books 2015
001

Written by Justin Richards
Illustrations by Dan Green
Copyright © BBC Worldwide Limited, 2015

Printed in China

A CIP catalogue record for this book is available from the British Library

ISBN: 978-1-405-92003-2

DOCTOR WHO

THE DANGEROUS BOOK OF

MONSTERS

CONTENTS

Introduction............... 6

The Daleks................. 8

The Emperor Dalek.......... 10

The Cult of Skaro.......... 12

Human Dalek Sec............ 14

Pig Slaves................. 15

The Ogrons................. 16

Dalekised Humans........... 17

Special Weapons Dalek...... 18

The Dalek Supreme.......... 19

Davros..................... 20

The New Dalek Paradigm..... 22

Creatures of The Time War . 23

The Hath................... 24

Fog Shark.................. 25

Clockwork Robots........... 26

Half-Face Man.............. 27

Robots of Sherwood......... 28

The Teller................. 30

The Skovox Blitzer......... 32

Dream Crabs................ 33

The Foretold............... 34

Akhaten Mummy.............. 36

Sutekh..................... 37

The Beast.................. 38

The Dæmons................. 39

Ood........................ 40

Werewolf................... 42

Carrionites................ 44

The Minotaur............... 46

Saturnynes................. 48

Haemovores................. 50

Plasmavore................. 51

Judoon..................... 52

Spoonheads................. 54

Lazarus Creature........... 55

The Boneless............... 56

Giant Spiders.............. 57

Spider Germs............... 58

Racnoss.................... 59

Stingrays.................. 60

Tritovores................. 61

Catkind.................... 62

Krillitanes................ 64

Midnight Entity............ 66

Krafayis................... 67

Vespiform.................. 68

Macra...................... 69

Winders and Smilers........ 70

Cybermen................... 72

Cyber Controller........... 74

Cybershades................ 76

CyberKing.................. 77

Cybermats.................. 78

Cyber-Doctor............... 80

Cybermites................. 81

3W Cybermen................ 82

Nestene Consciousness...... 84

Autons..................... 86

Cassandra.................. 88

Robot Spiders.............. 89

Visitors to Platform One... 90

Graske.................... 91
The Master................ 92
Missy..................... 94
Futurekind................ 96
The Toclafane............. 97
The Gelth................. 98
The Jagaroth.............. 99
The Dream Lord............ 100
Eknodines................. 101
Axons..................... 102
Handbots.................. 103
Slitheen.................. 104
Gas-Mask Zombies.......... 106
The Sycorax............... 108
Roboforms................. 109
The Jagrafess............. 110
The Wire.................. 111
Hoix...................... 112
The Krynoid............... 113
The Zygons................ 114
Elemental Shade........... 116
Abzorbaloff............... 117
Vashta Nerada............. 118
Spacesuit Zombies......... 119
The Sun-Possessed......... 120
Time Zombies.............. 121
Isolus.................... 122
Mr Sweet.................. 123
The Family of Blood....... 124
Scarecrows................ 126
Gantok.................... 127
Weeping Angels............ 128
Max Capricorn............. 130

Heavenly Host............. 131
Adipose................... 132
Draconians................ 133
Sontarans................. 134
Reapers................... 136
Terileptils............... 137
Time Beetle............... 138
Pyrovile.................. 139
The Flood................. 140
The Ice Warriors.......... 142
The Silurians............. 144
The Sea Devils............ 146
Dinosaurs................. 148
Solomon's Robots.......... 150
House..................... 151
The Shakri................ 152
Prisoner Zero............. 154
Silents................... 156
The Siren................. 158
Sil....................... 160
Headless Monks............ 161
Teselecta................. 162
Peg Dolls................. 164
The Terrible Zodin........ 165
Gangers................... 166
The Gunslinger............ 168
The Great Intelligence.... 170
Snowmen................... 172
The Yeti.................. 173
The Whisper Men........... 174
The Final Word............ 176

RIGHT, READ THIS CAREFULLY.

YES, EVEN YOU.

IT'S FOR YOUR BENEFIT.

THERE ARE SOME CORNERS OF THE UNIVERSE THAT HAVE BRED THE MOST TERRIBLE THINGS. The most dangerous monsters. If you want to have any hope of surviving an encounter with any of these monsters or living through an invasion, then this is the book for you.

This is the book where I'm going to tell you all about those monsters. Well, maybe not all about them. That would take far too long, and besides I have to keep some secrets. What's the point of being so old and wise and experienced and clever if someone else - like you - can just come along and read it all in a book?

But I'll tell you enough to survive.
If you're lucky. I hope.

I'll tell you about almost all the most dangerous monsters. I'll describe them to you, and if that's too difficult there are pictures too. I'll tell you how big they are, how fast they are, and how dangerous they are. Got that? Dangerous. Most important of all, I'll give you some hints and tips on how to survive if you happen to meet one.

Of course, the only really certain way of surviving when the monsters arrive is if I'm there. But even for a time-travelling genius that isn't always going to be possible. Sorry. So this book is your second-best chance. Keep it handy at all times. You never know when the monsters might be coming.

Don't just wait for them to arrive though, will you? There may not be time to whip out your handy guide, flick through to the right section, read it, and decide on a course of action before the claws or laser beams or death rays or jets of deadly ice cream strike. Well, maybe not the ice cream, but you get the idea.

SO DO YOUR HOMEWORK.
READ THIS BOOK.
AND ABOVE ALL, DO AS
I TELL YOU. ALWAYS.

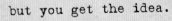

THE DOCTOR

THE DALEKS

NASTY, BUBBLING LUMPS OF HATE INSIDE
AN ARMOURED LIFE-SUPPORT SYSTEM.
NOTHING TO LIKE. Almost impossible to
stop. They just want to exterminate everyone,
which frankly suggests to me they have what
humans call an 'attitude
problem'. Think of your
worst nightmare - your
very worst ever. Daleks
are even worse.

These bulbs
light up when a
Dalek speaks.

EYE STALK - if the Dalek
has a weak point, this is it.

GUN - being shot
by a Dalek is not nice,
believe me.

It's probably just as well that Daleks hide inside their armoured casings - because this is what they really look like. Or nearly; this is just a sketch. The actual Dalek creature is far more disgusting and unpleasant than this.

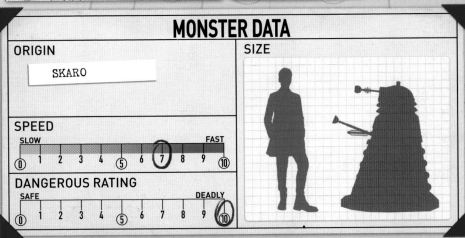

MONSTER DATA

ORIGIN

SKARO

SIZE

SPEED

SLOW   FAST

0 1 2 3 4 5 6 7 8 9 10

DANGEROUS RATING

SAFE   DEADLY

0 1 2 3 4 5 6 7 8 9 10

THE EMPEROR DALEK

DALEKS LIKE BEING TOLD WHAT TO DO. Not by you or me, but by other Daleks. At the top of the chain of command they've had the Dalek Supreme, Davros, and even a Dalek parliament and prime minister. But until the Time War, the Big Boss Dalek was the Emperor: huge, impressive, built into the Dalek City or Command Ship, and really, really nasty.

The top dome and eye stalk are a bit like an ordinary Dalek.

HUGE.

APPENDAGE FOR DETAIL SEE

The actual, real Emperor Dalek Creature is inside this transparent tank. He can see out, so you could wave to him. No, don't ACTUALLY wave to him. STOP THAT!

SURVIVAL TIPS

Remember what I said about not being able to survive a meeting with a Dalek? Similar advice here, I'm afraid. All right, so the Emperor is a bit immobile. But he has imperial guard Daleks - with darker-coloured domes - who will happily exterminate you on sight.

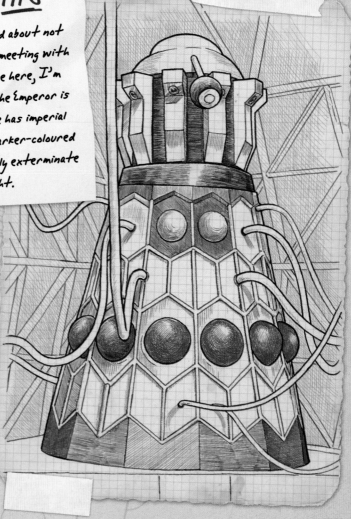

There have been several Emperor Daleks. When this one was destroyed - by me - they built a new one. Which also got destroyed. Also by me. Persistent things, Daleks. But they never learn.

MONSTER DATA

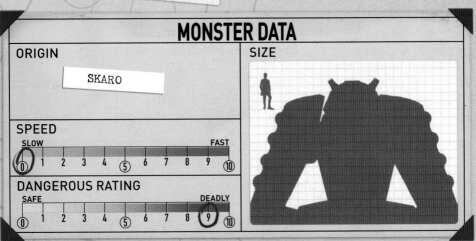

ORIGIN

SKARO

SIZE

SPEED

SLOW									FAST
0	1	2	3	4	5	6	7	8	9	10

DANGEROUS RATING

SAFE									DEADLY
0	1	2	3	4	5	6	7	8	9	10

THE CULT OF SKARO

BACK IN THE TIME WAR, THE DALEK EMPEROR SET UP A GROUP OF DALEKS WHO WERE TOLD TO THINK LIKE THE ENEMY. They were called the Cult of Skaro, and they dared to imagine. They even had names - Sec, Thay, Jast and Caan. I thought they were a myth - we all did. Until I met them. Not a happy meeting.

DALEK THAY.

DALEK SEC - the leader.

DALEK JAST.

DALEK CAAN was the last survivor of the Cult of Skaro - dropped back through time to rescue Davros.

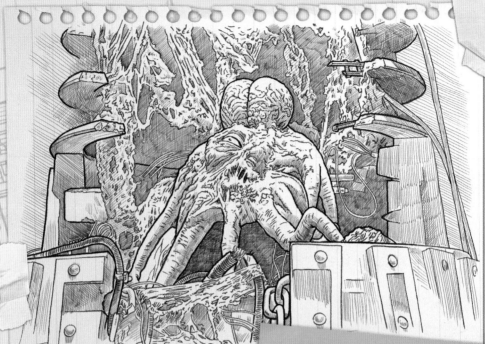

Dalek Caan used an emergency temporal shift to escape from New York in 1930, and went back into the Time War. He rescued Davros, the creator of the Daleks, but was badly damaged by the Time Vortex. After that he could predict the future, and that's never a good idea.

SURVIVAL TIPS

Daleks, extermination, no point in running or hiding – we've been through all this. But at least the Cult of Skaro is a bit more likely to listen when you plead for mercy; they're always trying to learn from their enemies. Pleading won't do you any good though. They'll still exterminate you.

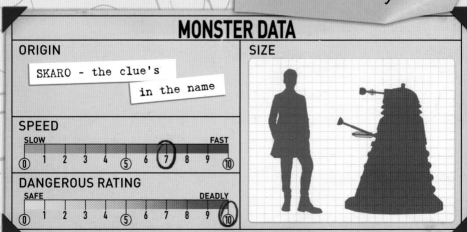

MONSTER DATA

ORIGIN

SKARO – the clue's in the name

SIZE

SPEED

SLOW   FAST

0   1   2   3   4   5   6   (7)   8   9   10

DANGEROUS RATING

SAFE   DEADLY

0   1   2   3   4   5   6   7   8   9   (10)

HUMAN DALEK SEC

DALEK SEC, LEADER OF THE CULT OF
SKARO, HAD THIS BRILLIANT IDEA -
BONKERS IDEA, MORE LIKE -
TO MERGE WITH A HUMAN.
The result was part human, part
Dalek, and completely grotesque.
The other Daleks in the Cult
of Skaro exterminated him
for being impure.

Head like a Dalek – tentacles, big brain, single eye.

Nice suit, although it could do with a clean.

SURVIVAL TIPS

This was a Dalek – or sort of Dalek – you could actually reason with. Problem was, as soon as the other Daleks worked that out, he was done for. Bye-bye, Sec. Pity, really.

MONSTER DATA

ORIGIN

SKARO - or, to be completely
accurate, half Skaro and half Earth

SPEED

SLOW										FAST
0	1	2	3	4	5	6	7	8	9	10

DANGEROUS RATING

SAFE										DEADLY
0	1	2	3	4	5	6	7	8	9	10

SIZE

PIG SLAVES

WHAT IS IT WITH PIGS? The Slitheen made a Space Pig, and in 1930s New York the Daleks made Pig Slaves. Half human, half pig, all bizarre. And unpleasant. Worse than being half Dalek.

It's a pig. Standing upright, but still a pig. Look at it: **PIG**.

Not very talkative, Pig Slaves. Lots of oink and that's about it.

SURVIVAL TIPS

Pig Slaves are quite sneaky, keeping to the shadows. If you're unlucky enough to catch sight of one, find somewhere brightly lit with lots of people, and you'll probably be safe. I think.

MONSTER DATA

ORIGIN

EARTH - New York, 1930

SIZE

SPEED

SLOW										FAST
0	1	2	3	4	5	6	7	8	9	10

DANGEROUS RATING

SAFE										DEADLY
0	1	2	3	4	5	6	7	8	9	10

THE OGRONS

STRONG AND STUPID. The Ogrons are like giant apes, and used by other life-forms to do their dirty work. A big favourite of the Daleks - though Daleks don't really have 'favourites'. But they do use the Ogrons as security guards or expendable troops.

Ogrons will eat anything – won't even peel bananas.

They're usually armed. But, even if not, they're massively strong.

Top of the head is a weak point.

SURVIVAL TIPS

You'll know if there's an Ogron around. They barge in and thump. If you have to fight, try to bash them on the head – if you can reach. Short people like Clara have no chance.

MONSTER DATA

ORIGIN

THE OGRON HOMEWORLD - a name about as imaginative as the Ogrons themselves

SPEED

SLOW · · · · · FAST
⓪ 1 2 3 4 ⑤ 6 7 8 9 ⑩

DANGEROUS RATING

SAFE · · · · · DEADLY
⓪ 1 2 3 4 ⑤ 6 7 8 9 ⑩

SIZE

DALEKISED HUMANS

IS 'DALEKISED' A WORD? Never mind, it'll do. The Daleks 'dalekise' some people, and the bulky headgear is a clue. Dalekised humans are less conspicuous - until the Daleks take control. Then, a big Dalek eye stalk appears out of their forehead.

When under Dalek control, an eye stalk appears here – big clue.

You don't have to be alive to be controlled.

Actually, you're not alive. Trouble is, you don't know you're dead.

SURVIVAL TIPS

If someone's behaving oddly, check their forehead. If it glows blue and a Dalek eye stalk pokes out, that means trouble. They're already dead, so you can't kill them again. See if you can lock them away somewhere while you escape.

MONSTER DATA

ORIGIN

Wherever the Daleks found them

SIZE

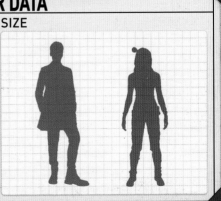

SPEED

SLOW   FAST
0 1 2 3 4 5 6 7 8 9 10

DANGEROUS RATING

SAFE   DEADLY
0 1 2 3 4 5 6 7 8 9 10

SPECIAL WEAPONS DALEK

THINK OF A DALEK CROSSED WITH A TANK. A Special
Weapons Dalek is only wheeled out when the big guns are needed
because, well, it has a big gun. Big Gun Dalek, they should
have called it.

No eye stalk or sucker arm.

Just a Big Gun. So big it can easily destroy other Daleks.

No pride in its appearance. Look: oil, dirt, grease...

⫶⫶⫶ SURVIVAL TIPS ⫶⫶⫶

Same as for other Daleks, really: forget
it. The Special Weapons Dalek is even less
talkative than the usual kind. But you'll
probably know when it's around, from the
sound of things blowing up. AVOID.

MONSTER DATA

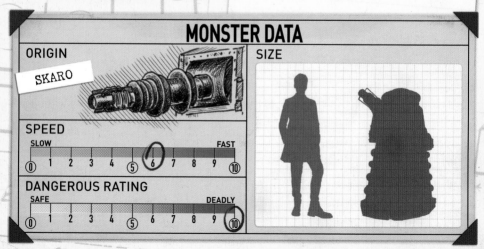

ORIGIN

SKARO

SIZE

SPEED

SLOW   FAST
⓪ 1 2 3 4 ⑤ 6 7 8 9 ⑩

DANGEROUS RATING

SAFE   DEADLY
⓪ 1 2 3 4 ⑤ 6 7 8 9 ⑩

THE DALEK SUPREME

HEAD OF THE DALEKS' SUPREME COUNCIL, THE DALEK SUPREME HAS HAD A FEW DESIGNS. A plain black paint job, a natty black-and-gold scheme, and this big red version with added chunky dome bits. Big Boss Dalek - not to be messed with.

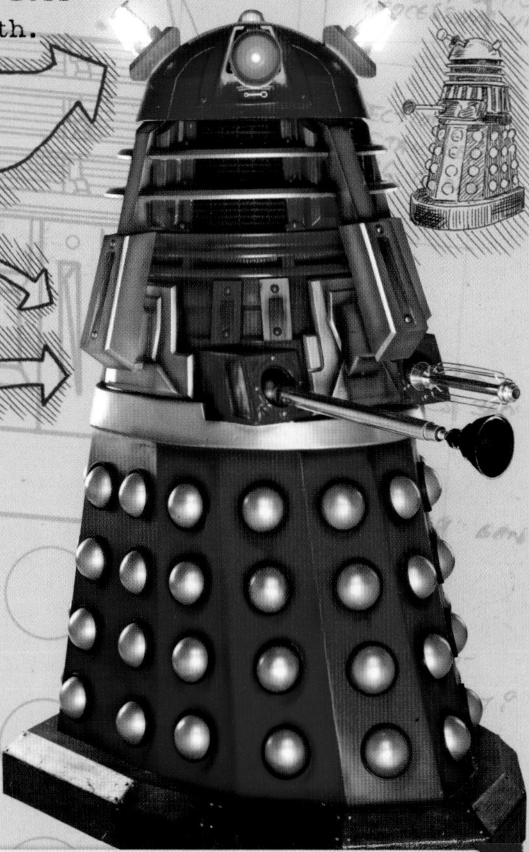

Bigger dome lights – it probably just wants to look important.

Chunkier top section.

Blood-red colour scheme. Well, that's appropriate.

SURVIVAL TIPS

The Dalek Supreme lurks amongst loads of other Daleks, giving orders and generally being bossy. So the only way you'll meet is if you've been captured already. Bit late to run now.

MONSTER DATA

ORIGIN

SKARO

SPEED

SLOW — FAST

0 1 2 3 4 5 6 7 8 9 10 (7 circled)

DANGEROUS RATING

SAFE — DEADLY

0 1 2 3 4 5 6 7 8 9 10 (10 circled)

SIZE

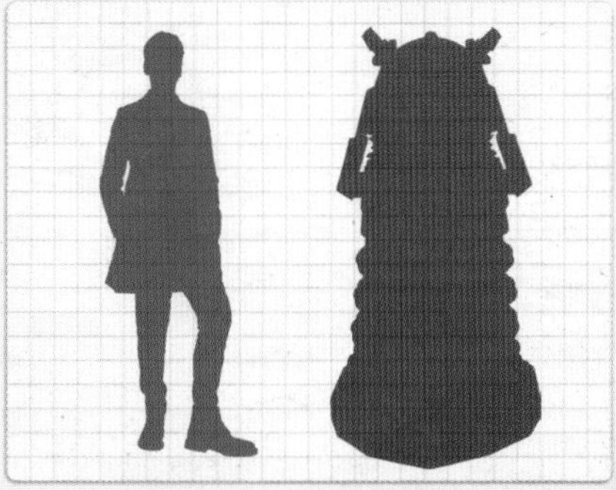

DAVROS

TALK ABOUT BANANAS. Davros was a Kaled scientist who discovered that the weapons used in a thousand-year war against the Thals were mutating his people into horrible blobby creatures. Does he try to stop the war and find a cure? No - he invents the Dalek to put the blobby mutants inside.

He has an electronic eye.

His only hand was shot off on planet Necros. He replaced it with a metal claw.

Davros's life-support system is like the base of a Dalek.

Davros worked out the final form the mutated Kaleds would take. Then he designed the Dalek as a travel machine for it, and tinkered with them to make them hate everything.
No wonder they turned on him . . .

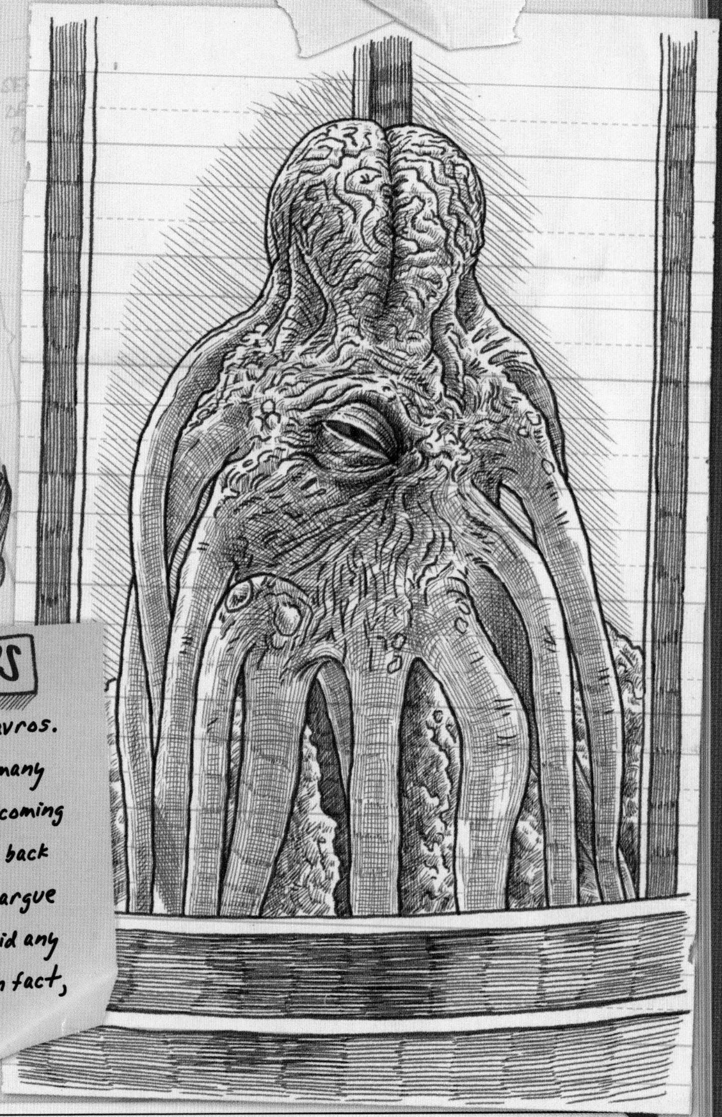

SURVIVAL TIPS

He's a slippery customer, Davros. He's been killed almost as many times as I have, but keeps coming back. He was even dragged back from the Time War. He can argue black is white, so I'd avoid any conversation with him. In fact, just avoid him.

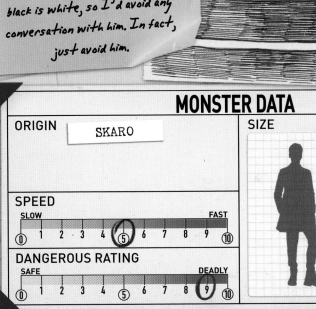

MONSTER DATA

ORIGIN

SKARO

SIZE

SPEED

SLOW   FAST

⓪ 1 2 3 4 ⑤ 6 7 8 9 ⑩

DANGEROUS RATING

SAFE   DEADLY

⓪ 1 2 3 4 ⑤ 6 7 8 ⑨ ⑩

THE NEW DALEK PARADIGM

CREATED FROM A PROGENITOR DEVICE LEFT BEHIND AFTER THE TIME WAR, THE NEW PARADIGM DALEKS ARE BIG AND COLOURFUL. Not sure why, but I guess you have to move with the times.

Scientist.

Supreme.

Strategist.

Eternal.

ALL NASTY.

Drone.

SURVIVAL TIPS

They might get a new paint job and alter what they look like, but a Dalek is a Dalek is a Dalek. They'll still exterminate you as soon as look at you. As with other Daleks, their eye stalk is their weakest spot: Aim there and it will buy you a minute or two to flee.

MONSTER DATA

ORIGIN

SKARO

SIZE

SPEED

SLOW — 0 1 2 3 4 5 6 7 8 9 10 — FAST

DANGEROUS RATING

SAFE — 0 1 2 3 4 5 6 7 8 9 10 — DEADLY

CREATURES OF THE TIME WAR

THERE WERE ALL SORTS OF HORRIFIC CREATURES THROWN UP BY THE TIME WAR: Skaro Degradations and the Nightmare Child, the Army of Meanwhiles and the Never-weres. If war is hell, then the Time War created Hell and the creatures that live there . . .

SURVIVAL TIPS

Even though it's over, the Time War can still kill you – that's how time paradoxes work. Best not to worry. Forget I mentioned it. It'll never happen . . .

The Never-weres — creatures that should never have existed.

Made of bits and pieces of evolution that never happened.

No nice cuddly fluffy bits, but plenty of teeth, spikes and claws.

MONSTER DATA

ORIGIN

Born out of the horrendous Time War between Daleks and Time Lords

SPEED

Variable - depends which of them you meet

SLOW | FAST
0 1 2 3 4 5 6 7 8 9 10

DANGEROUS RATING

SAFE | DEADLY
0 1 2 3 4 5 6 7 8 9 10

SIZE

?

Different creatures, different sizes - some are smaller than you can see, others the size of a planet. Or bigger

23

THE HATH

A GREAT BIG UPRIGHT FISH. In a spacesuit. Breathing oxygenated liquid. That's the Hath. Not usually dangerous, but I did get caught up in a war between the Hath and human colonists on the planet Messaline. Humans - always so petty!

GILLS - useless out of water. So the Hath breathes green liquid.

Re-breather filled with green liquid.

Not sure why they wear these overalls, but underneath they're probably green.

SURVIVAL TIPS

Some Hath have quite a temper, so be careful. Difficult to negotiate with, the Hath - since they talk through the liquid in their suits, it's all bubbles and gurgles.

MONSTER DATA

ORIGIN

Unknown

SPEED

SLOW ———————————————— FAST
0 1 2 3 4 5 6 7 8 9 10

DANGEROUS RATING

SAFE ———————————————— DEADLY
0 1 2 3 4 5 6 7 8 9 10

SIZE

FOG SHARK

THERE'S A PLANET CALLED EMBER WHERE THE FOG GETS SO THICK THAT FISH SWIM IN IT. No, really - fish. Little fish, not a problem. But some are quite big. And scary. With teeth. Like sharks. Well, not just like sharks - actually sharks. Swimming through the air.

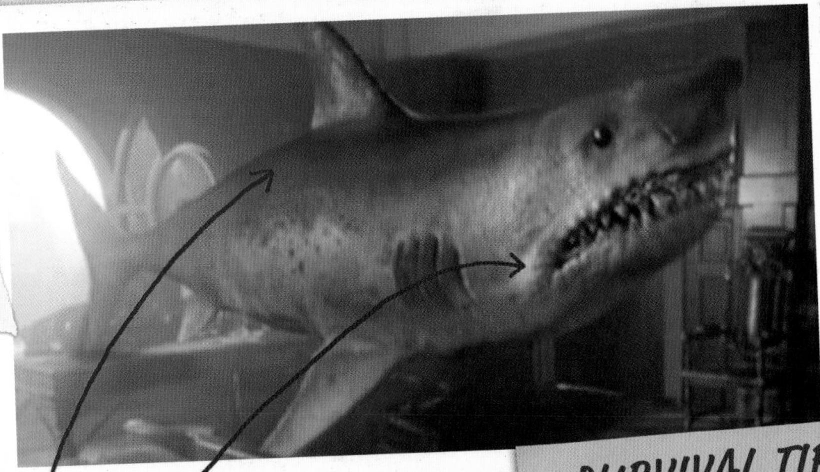

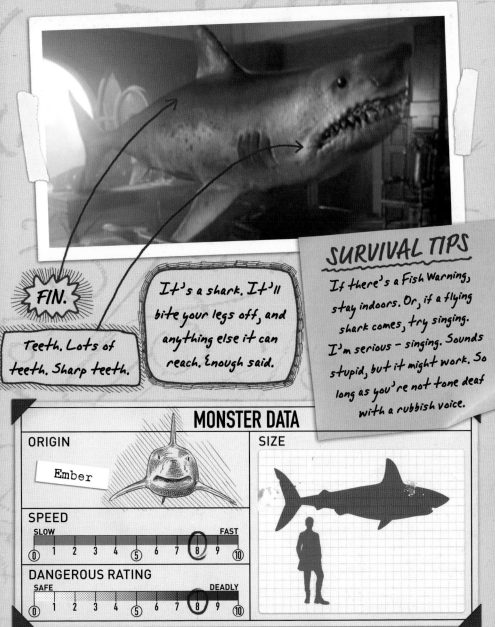

FIN.

Teeth. Lots of teeth. Sharp teeth.

It's a shark. It'll bite your legs off, and anything else it can reach. Enough said.

SURVIVAL TIPS

If there's a Fish Warning, stay indoors. Or, if a flying shark comes, try singing. I'm serious - singing. Sounds stupid, but it might work. So long as you're not tone deaf with a rubbish voice.

MONSTER DATA

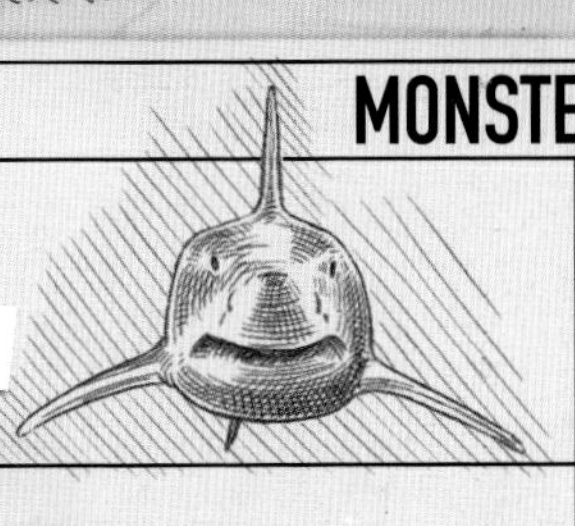

ORIGIN

Ember

SIZE

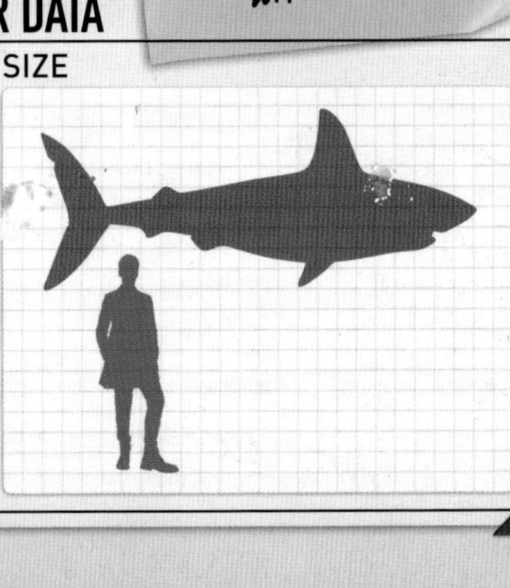

SPEED

SLOW — FAST

0 1 2 3 4 5 6 7 [8] 9 10

DANGEROUS RATING

SAFE — DEADLY

0 1 2 3 4 5 6 7 [8] 9 10

CLOCKWORK ROBOTS

IT'S A GOOD IDEA: have your repair robots run on clockwork and, if your spaceship's power fails, the robots can still repair it. The problems start when the robots decide to use parts of the crew to repair the systems.

Mask and wig hide the clockwork.

> This one is in disguise. It's off to eighteenth-century France because – well, because it's gone bonkers, quite frankly.

SURVIVAL TIPS

Clockwork robots try to hide by breaking your clock. So if you've got a broken clock but you can still hear it ticking, you might be in trouble. Multigrain anti-oil can cause them to seize up, so keep some handy.

MONSTER DATA

ORIGIN
Used on various ships including the *SS Madame de Pompadour* and the *SS Marie Antoinette*

SIZE

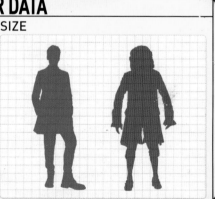

SPEED
SLOW 0 1 2 3 4 (5) 6 7 8 9 10 FAST

DANGEROUS RATING
SAFE 0 1 2 3 4 (5) 6 (7) 8 9 10 DEADLY

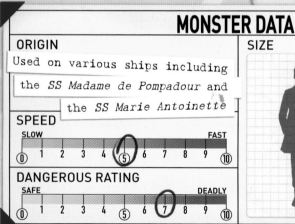

HALF-FACE MAN

I MET THIS CLOCKWORK MAN AND HIS CLOCKWORK MATES IN VICTORIAN LONDON AFTER THEIR SHIP CRASHED - LONG, LONG AFTER. I could tell he was clockwork because he only had half a face. Dead giveaway.

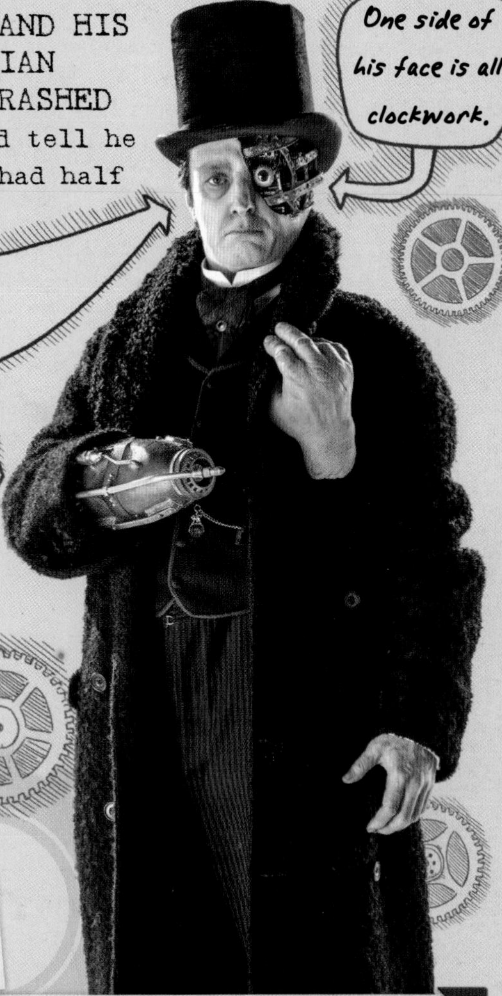

One side of his face is all clockwork.

Eyes don't match – since they came from different 'donors'.

Hands don't match either – and one can be replaced with a blowtorch.

SURVIVAL TIPS

The Half-Face Man tried to look human by covering himself with people's skin and stealing their eyes and hands and . . . You get the idea. He shouldn't give you any trouble, as he fell out of a flying restaurant. That's my story, anyway.

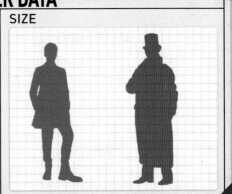

MONSTER DATA

ORIGIN

Spaceship *SS Marie Antoinette*

SIZE

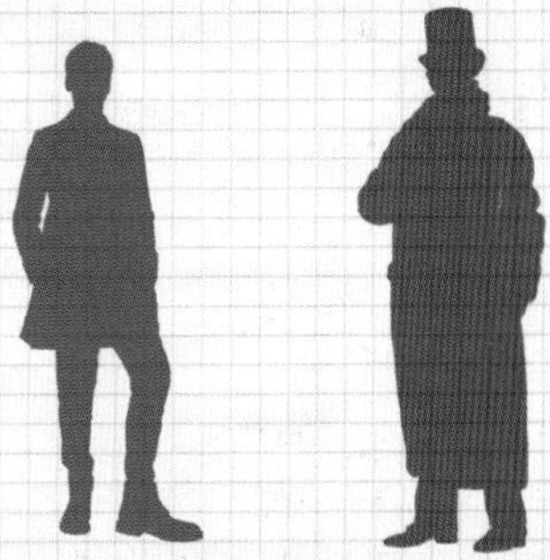

SPEED

SLOW — FAST

0 1 2 3 4 5 6 7 8 9 10 (5 circled)

DANGEROUS RATING

SAFE — DEADLY

0 1 2 3 4 5 6 7 8 9 10 (7 circled)

ROBOTS OF SHERWOOD

THE ROBOT CREW OF A SPACESHIP THAT CRASHED NEAR TWELFTH-CENTURY NOTTINGHAM. They disguised themselves as knights and got the Sheriff of Nottingham to help them get gold to seal an engine breach, killing anyone who opposed them. Dodgy lot, really. Had to get help from Robin Hood for this one - well, he *claimed* he was Robin Hood.

> Disguised as a knight in armour - not too tricky, as both are made of metal.

> Helmet opens to show the robot inside - and so it can shoot a laser from its eyes.

> Not very talkative. Often the way with robots, no conversation.

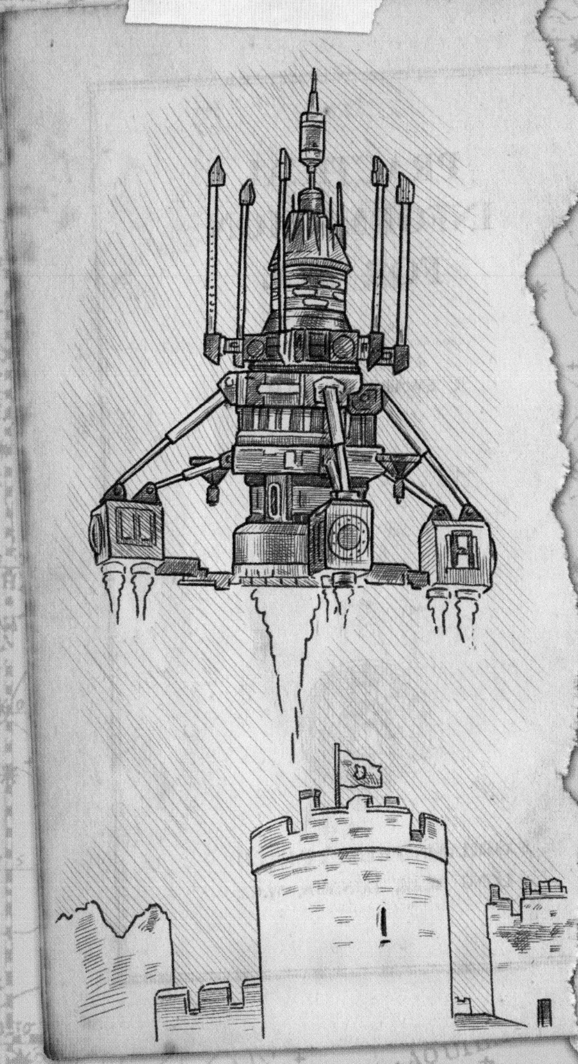

No one noticed a spaceship disguised as a dirty great castle arriving in the middle of the countryside . . . But they certainly noticed it when it took off again. Not that it got very far. Luckily I managed to get it into orbit before it exploded, so no one underneath got hurt.

SURVIVAL TIPS

Be careful if you meet a knight in armour whose helmet opens up and has a robot's head inside. Fortunately, they're not too bright – unlike the lasers they fire from their eyes. But if you have something shiny you can use to reflect the laser back at them, then **BANG!**

MONSTER DATA

ORIGIN

Unknown, but they were heading for 'The Promised Land', wherever that is.

SPEED

SLOW 0 1 2 3 4 5 (6) 7 8 9 10 FAST

DANGEROUS RATING

SAFE 0 1 2 3 4 5 6 (7) 8 9 10 DEADLY

SIZE

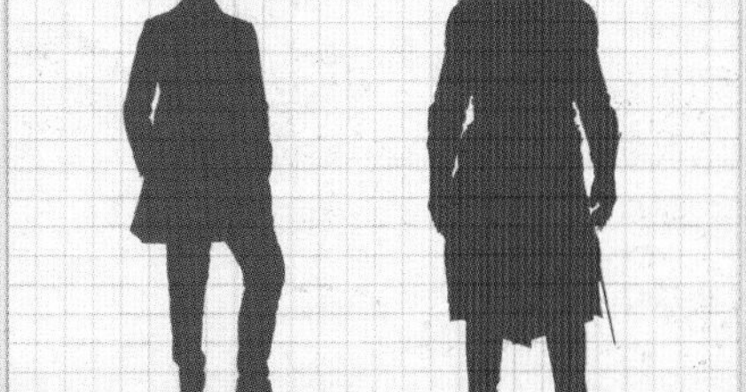

THE TELLER

THE TELLER WAS USED BY THE BANK OF KARABRAXOS TO SPOT ANYONE WITH CRIMINAL INTENT. It can scan your thoughts and tell if you're up to no good. Then it turns your brain into soup. Not the sort of soup you eat with crusty bread. Oh, no.

It had the power to liquefy guilty people's brains.

The Teller was kept apart from the only other surviving member of its race.

It could tell whether you were up to no good – hence the nickname. No idea what its real name was. Probably Kevin.

The Bank of Karabraxos was impossible to break into. But someone managed. Several someones, actually, led by yours truly. We thought we'd been sent there by some criminal mastermind. Turned out the mastermind who'd sent us there was *me* - to rescue the Teller. Funny how things work out sometimes, isn't it?

MONSTER DATA

ORIGIN

Unknown

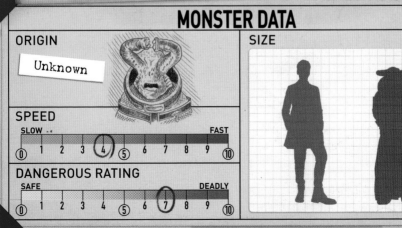

SPEED

SLOW ⟶ FAST
0 1 2 3 4 5 6 7 8 9 10

DANGEROUS RATING

SAFE ⟶ DEADLY
0 1 2 3 4 5 6 7 8 9 10

SIZE

THE SKOVOX BLITZER

AN ALIEN MILITARY KILLING MACHINE FROM A DISTANT WAR. A Skovox Blitzer has enough explosives in its built-in armoury to take out a whole planet. They can home in on artron energy, which isn't good because I'm full of it.

Eyes can detect infra-red radiation.

Mobility unit - looks like a robot in a wheelchair, but it's nippy enough.

SURVIVAL TIPS

A Skovox Blitzer is one of the deadliest killing machines ever. Running away fast is highly recommended. If nothing else, you'll at least be a bit fitter and healthier when you die.

Weapons in arms.

Packed with explosives.

MONSTER DATA

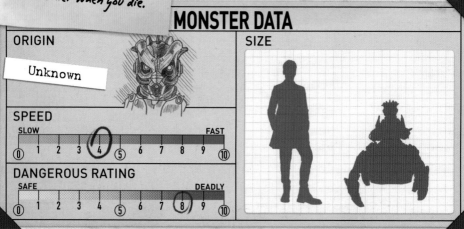

ORIGIN

Unknown

SPEED

SLOW | 0 1 2 3 4 5 6 7 8 9 10 | FAST

DANGEROUS RATING

SAFE | 0 1 2 3 4 5 6 7 8 9 10 | DEADLY

SIZE

DREAM CRABS

NOT NICE AT ALL. A Dream Crab attaches to your face and digests you. But, to stop you realising what's happening, it gives you *dreams*. It makes you think you're somewhere happy and everything's all right. But it's not - you're dying. Sorry.

Dream Crabs clamp themselves over your face.

Then they eat your brain.

They induce dreams of well-being, relax you, make you feel at ease . . .

SURVIVAL TIPS

If a Dream Crab gets you, you'll feel a slight pain in the head, like you've just eaten very cold ice cream. If you have, that's fine. But if not - WAKE UP!!

MONSTER DATA

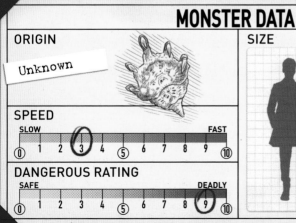

ORIGIN

Unknown

SPEED

SLOW 0 1 2 (3) 4 5 6 7 8 9 10 FAST

DANGEROUS RATING

SAFE 0 1 2 3 4 5 6 7 8 (9) 10 DEADLY

SIZE

THE FORETOLD

THE LEGEND OF THE FORETOLD HAS BEEN AROUND FOR THOUSANDS OF YEARS. The Foretold was a mummy - rotting corpse, decaying bandages, the whole deal. Only, if you see it, then exactly sixty-six seconds later you'll die. No ifs, no buts. That's it - you'll be dead as a dodo.

Corpse of a soldier, wrapped in bandages.

Its body's been engineered so it won't ever die.

It thinks it's still fighting the war - get in the way and you're an enemy, soon to be kaput.

SURVIVAL TIPS

Only one person's ever survived: me. It was on the Orient Express – the one in space – and, once I realised it was an enhanced, undead soldier, it was easy. I surrendered. Not what I'd usually do when faced with a monster, but in this case it's what anyone should do.

The Foretold was a soldier left over from some war no one remembers. Enhanced and filled with technology, it couldn't die. And it thought it was still fighting the war - defending the flag of its people. It selected the weakest victims first, and then worked its way through, well, everyone else around it.

MONSTER DATA

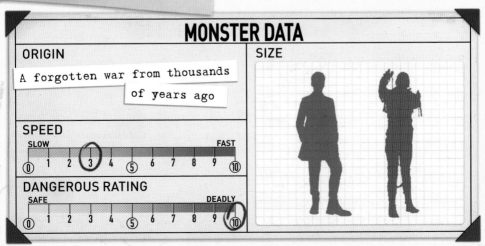

ORIGIN

A forgotten war from thousands of years ago

SPEED

SLOW – FAST

0 1 2 3 4 5 6 7 8 9 10 (3 circled)

DANGEROUS RATING

SAFE – DEADLY

0 1 2 3 4 5 6 7 8 9 10 (10 circled)

SIZE

AKHATEN MUMMY

THIS MUMMY LOOKED REAL ENOUGH BUT WAS, IN FACT, AN ALARM CLOCK. Sounds daft, but there it is. It was sleeping in a pyramid on an asteroid above the planet Akhaten, which wasn't a planet after all but a hungry creature waiting for the mummy to wake it up.

Ancient creature – no wonder I thought it was the Old God. Big mistake.

Different alien races presented gifts to it at the Festival of Offerings.

Singing kept it asleep. Mostly.

SURVIVAL TIPS

If the Mummy wakes then, to lull it back to sleep, you need to give up something of great personal value. I can't tell you what exactly, because everyone will have something different to give...

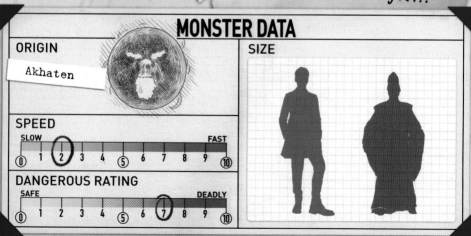

MONSTER DATA

ORIGIN

Akhaten

SIZE

SPEED

SLOW   FAST
0 1 2 3 4 5 6 7 8 9 10

DANGEROUS RATING

SAFE   DEADLY
0 1 2 3 4 5 6 7 8 9 10

SUTEKH

THE ANCIENT EGYPTIANS THOUGHT THAT THE ALIEN OSIRANS WERE GODS. Sutekh was an evil warmonger who the other Osirans imprisoned in a tomb beneath a pyramid. But he used Osiran service robots - which look like walking Egyptian mummies - to try to escape.

Sutekh was imprisoned beneath a pyramid and unable to move.

But his psychic power helped him control others.

SURVIVAL TIPS

I aged Sutekh to death in a time tunnel. But if you come across an Osiran servicer you'll need a Control Ring to order it to return to Control. Though they're not easy to come by. Good luck!

Beneath the mask, Sutekh's head was like a giant jackal.

MONSTER DATA

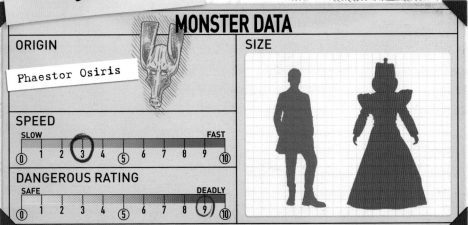

ORIGIN

Phaestor Osiris

SIZE

SPEED

SLOW ——————— FAST
0 1 2 3 4 5 6 7 8 9 10

DANGEROUS RATING

SAFE ——————— DEADLY
0 1 2 3 4 5 6 7 8 9 10

THE BEAST

THE BEAST IS THE *ORIGINAL* MONSTER. It was there before time itself existed, if you can imagine that - I find it difficult. Fortunately, the Disciples of the Light imprisoned it at the core of a planet that was orbiting a black hole. Unfortunately, that didn't stop it trying to break free.

Horns - an ancient symbol of power.

Blood red in colour - that can't be a coincidence.

Shoots fire from its mouth.

The Beast doesn't look like all those stereotypical demons - they all look like the Beast!

SURVIVAL TIPS

The Beast is so powerful even its mind could escape and possess others. If you come over all strange with runes written across your face, you're in trouble. You'd better just hope I'm there to save you.

MONSTER DATA

ORIGIN

It existed before anything else

SPEED

SLOW 0 1 2 3 4 5 6 7 8 9 10 FAST

UNKNOWN

DANGEROUS RATING

SAFE 0 1 2 3 4 5 6 7 8 9 10 DEADLY

(10 circled)

SIZE

THE DÆMONS

THE DÆMONS CAME TO EARTH 100,000 YEARS AGO AND HELPED HUMANITY TO EVOLVE. For the Dæmons it was an experiment: if they thought humans were a disaster - which, let's be honest, is one interpretation - they'd destroy everyone.

They have the power to shrink or grow.

The typical image of a demon is based on ancient memories of the Dæmons.

SURVIVAL TIPS

Best steer clear of black magic as that could summon a Dæmon or, in fact, a demon. Dæmons are Big Trouble, but, so long as you're not a complete pudding-brain, you can confuse them as they are very logical and can't stand paradoxes.

MONSTER DATA

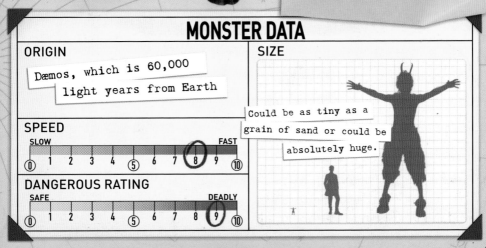

ORIGIN

Dæmos, which is 60,000 light years from Earth

SPEED

SLOW — 0 1 2 3 4 (5) 6 7 **8** 9 10 — FAST

DANGEROUS RATING

SAFE — 0 1 2 3 4 (5) 6 7 8 **9** 10 — DEADLY

SIZE

Could be as tiny as a grain of sand or could be absolutely huge.

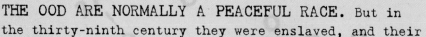

THE OOD ARE NORMALLY A PEACEFUL RACE. But in the thirty-ninth century they were enslaved, and their hindbrains were removed and replaced with translation spheres. All of which is fine (well, not the brain removal and slavery, obviously, but I've sorted that out now) unless an Ood gets red-eye - then they turn rabid and extremely dangerous.

Watch out for red or green eyes.

No mouth - hence the need for the translation sphere.

Make an Ood angry and they'll electrocute you.

An Ood actually has three brains: the forebrain in its head; the hindbrain, which it normally carries in its hands; and the giant hive brain, which is kept beneath the surface of their planet, and to which all Ood are telepathically connected.

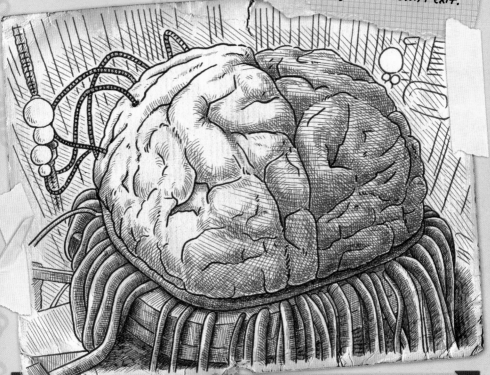

MONSTER DATA

ORIGIN

The Ood-Sphere

SPEED

SLOW — FAST

0 1 2 3 4 5 6 7 8 9 10

DANGEROUS RATING

SAFE — DEADLY

0 1 2 3 4 5 6 7 8 9 10

SIZE

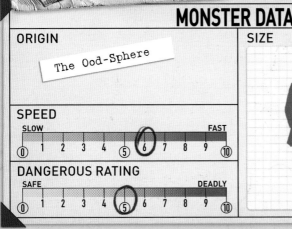

WEREWOLF

IN 1540, A LUPINE WAVELENGTH HAEMOVARIFORM FELL TO
EARTH IN A REMOTE PART OF SCOTLAND. It modelled itself
on local legends, turning its human host into a werewolf every
full moon. It wanted to bite Queen Victoria. She was not
amused, I can assure you.

Looks like a proper werewolf -
fur, teeth, claws, the lot.

Prince Albert knew of the
werewolf and set a trap for
it using a huge diamond.

SURVIVAL TIPS

If it's not a full moon, you're probably OK. But, if it is, and someone is acting a bit weird and their eyes go black . . . Well, you get the idea. Mistletoe can keep a werewolf at bay. Or simply hit the beast with magnified moonlight – it will drown in too much of the stuff.

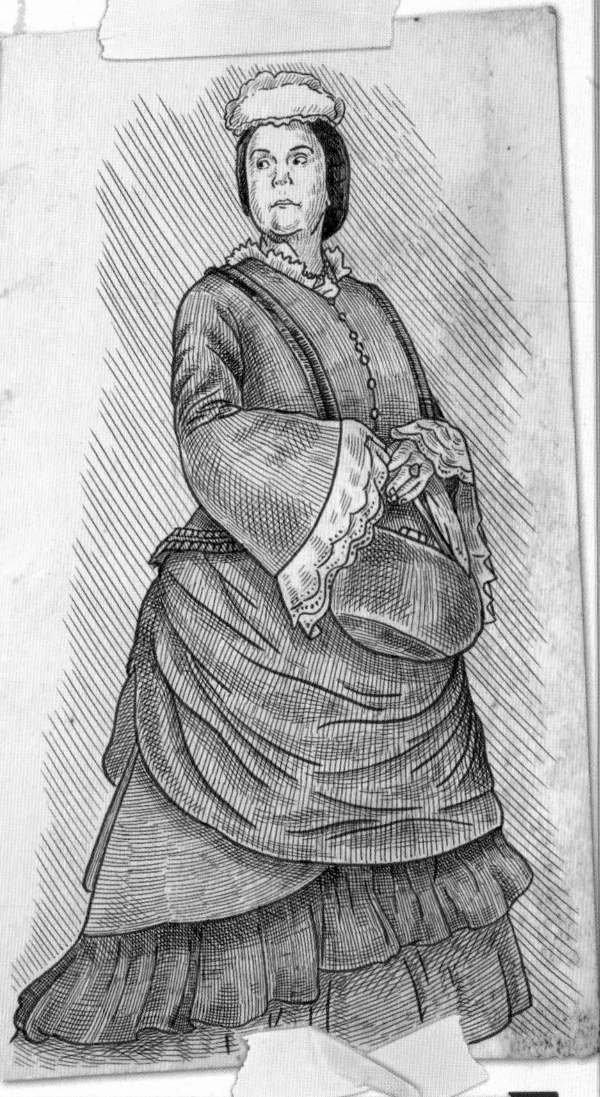

The werewolf attacked Queen Victoria in Scotland in 1879, hoping to turn her into a werewolf as well, and take over the British Empire. But I used a massive diamond and a telescope to stop it. Saved the Empire - just saying. Not that Victoria was grateful - she had me banished. *Me!*

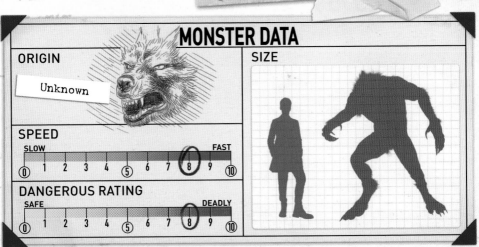

MONSTER DATA

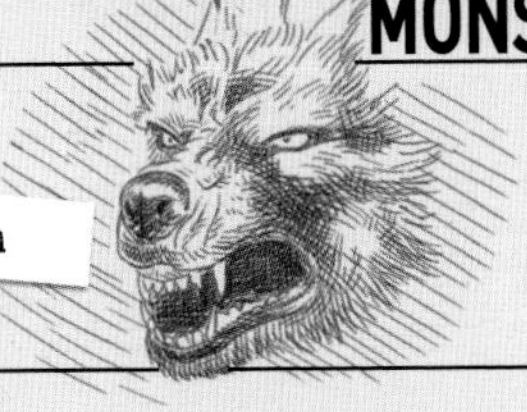

ORIGIN

Unknown

SPEED

SLOW 0 1 2 3 4 5 6 7 (8) 9 10 FAST

DANGEROUS RATING

SAFE 0 1 2 3 4 5 6 7 (8) 9 10 DEADLY

SIZE

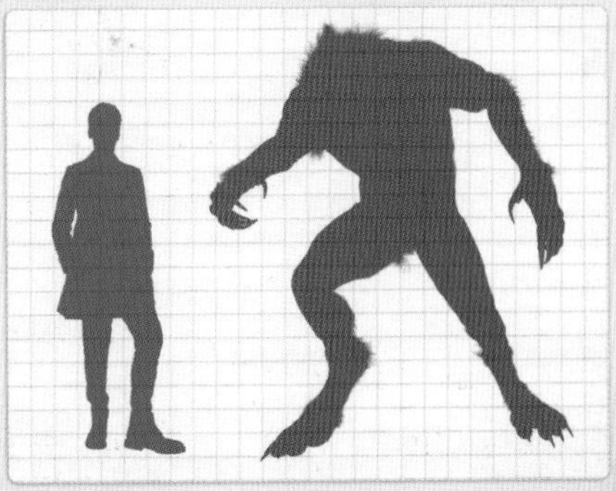

CARRIONITES

MOST LIFEFORMS UNDERSTAND THE UNIVERSE BY NUMBERS - MATHS AND SCIENCE AND STUFF.

But the Carrionites used *words*. Their formulae seemed like spells. They were banished to the Deep Darkness by the Eternals long ago, though some escaped through a lost Shakespeare play and tried to feed on the world. Long story.

Don't let this one touch your heart or it will stop ticking.

Don't they EVER cut their fingernails?

The three Carrionites who escaped into Elizabethan London were Mother Doomfinger, Mother Bloodtide, and Lilith.

These three escaped Carrionites used a combination of Shakespeare's brilliant words and the shape of the newly built Globe Theatre to free the other Carrionites from the Deep Darkness. Didn't work though - someone incredibly clever (guess who) changed the end of the play so they got imprisoned again.

The Globe

MONSTER DATA

ORIGIN

Rexel 4

SIZE

SPEED

SLOW   FAST
0 1 2 3 4 5 6 7 8 9 10

DANGEROUS RATING

SAFE   DEADLY
0 1 2 3 4 5 6 7 8 9 10

THE MINOTAUR

THE MINOTAUR WAS IMPRISONED IN A SPACESHIP THAT SEEMED LIKE A HOTEL. (A real hotel would lose a star for that.) The Minotaur was probably one of a race that moved from planet to planet, expecting to be worshipped as gods and feeding on people's faith. But one race resisted and locked him up.

Looks like the mythical Minotaur.

Actually, I did meet the mythical Minotaur, too, back in ancient Atlantis. But that's another story.

And the Nimon – they were a bit like Minotaurs, too.

This particular Minotaur feeds on faith.

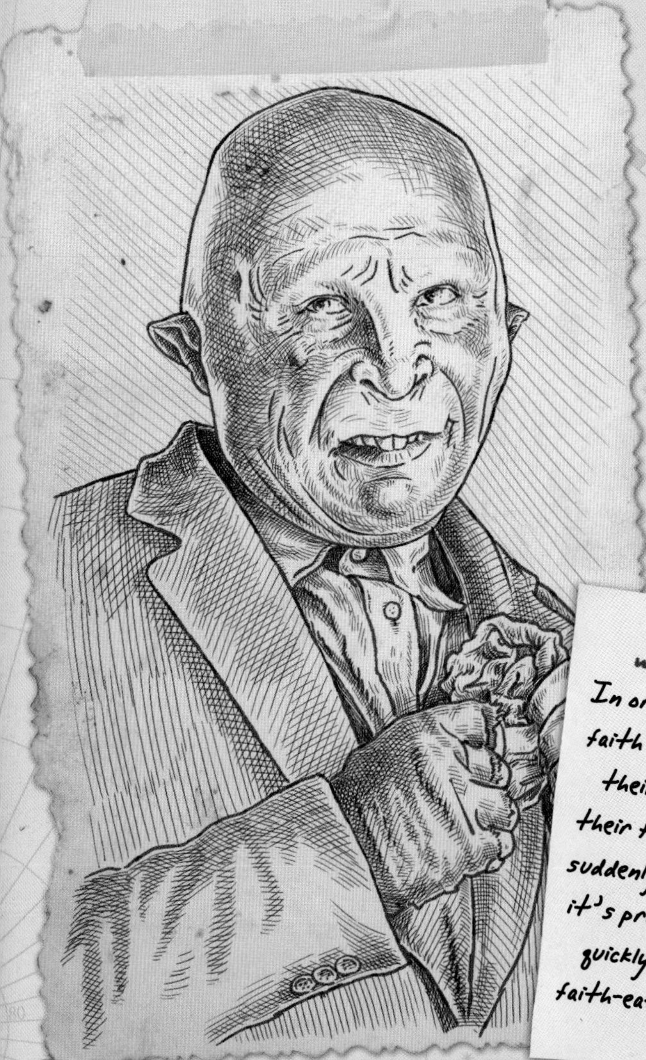

The people in the 'hotel' were brought there as food for the imprisoned Minotaur. They were quite a weird assortment - the weirdest was probably Gibbis. He was a Tivolian. They're instinctively cowardly, and Gibbis was no exception - his school motto was 'Resistance is exhausting'.

SURVIVAL TIPS

In order to discover what people had faith in, the Minotaur showed people their worst fears. Then it fed on their faith, and killed them. So, if you suddenly find the thing you fear most, it's probably a good idea to move along quickly - whether there's an alien faith-eating Minotaur around or not.

MONSTER DATA

ORIGIN

Unknown

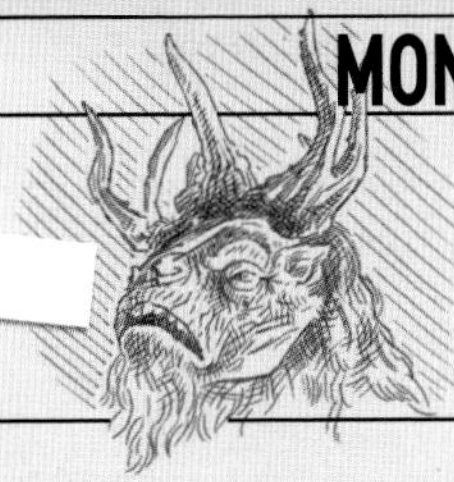

SIZE

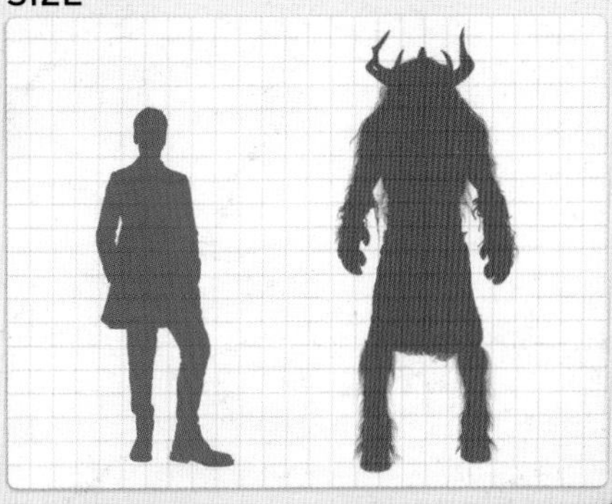

SPEED

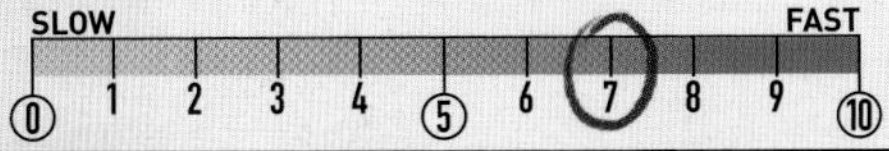

SLOW
FAST
0 1 2 3 4 5 6 7 8 9 10

DANGEROUS RATING

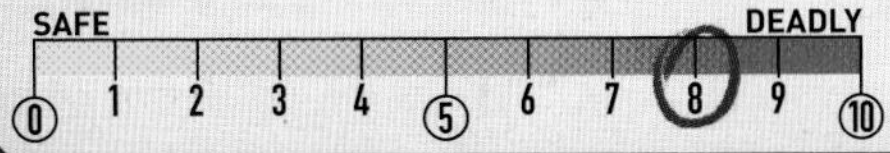

SAFE
DEADLY
0 1 2 3 4 5 6 7 8 9 10

VAMPIRE FISH FROM SPACE - HOW BONKERS IS THAT? One Saturnyne female arrived in Venice in the sixteenth century and started to convert local women into vampire brides for her sons beneath the water. She planned to sink Venice, too, so they'd have somewhere nice to live. Not so good for everyone else, of course. Venice is quite wet enough as it is.

The Venetian Saturnyne called herself Rosanna Calvierri.

She used a perception filter to hide her true appearance.

Big teeth, whether in fish form or as a 'human' vampire, are always an indication that things may not be quite right.

Rosanna Calvierri ran a school for young women. But she was actually gathering brides for her 10,000 alien-fish children. I stopped her but, sadly, it was too late to save most of the girls from being turned into vampires. The weddings were off. Just as well - imagine sorting out the menu.

MONSTER DATA

ORIGIN

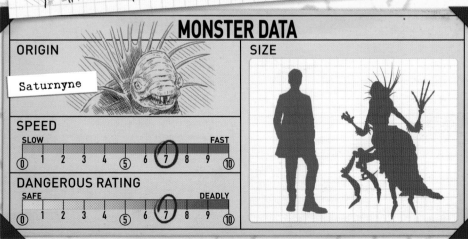

Saturnyne

SPEED

SLOW   FAST
0 1 2 3 4 5 6 7 8 9 10

DANGEROUS RATING

SAFE   DEADLY
0 1 2 3 4 5 6 7 8 9 10

SIZE

HAEMOVORES

THERE'S A CREATURE OF ANCIENT EVIL CALLED FENRIC. If he had his way, the human race would eventually evolve into Haemovores - revolting grey vampire creatures, covered in nodules and suckers, that feed on blood.

People from throughout history became Haemovores.

Fenric planned to infect the seas with pollution from the future.

Talk about complicated. But time paradoxes work like that.

SURVIVAL TIPS

If there are Haemovores around, don't go into the water . . . though they can come and get you on land as well. Faith can hold them off – so have faith in something, and cling to that.

MONSTER DATA

ORIGIN

Earth (in a future that probably won't happen - let's hope)

SPEED

SLOW — FAST

0 1 2 3 4 5 6 7 8 9 10 (6 circled)

DANGEROUS RATING

SAFE — DEADLY

0 1 2 3 4 5 6 7 8 9 10 (8 circled)

SIZE

PLASMAVORE

THE ALIEN PLASMAVORE THAT MARTHA AND I ENCOUNTERED WAS DISGUISED AS A LITTLE OLD LADY CALLED FLORENCE.

Just shows - appearances can be deceptive. She'd already killed the Child Princess of Padrivole Regency Nine by sucking her blood.

SURVIVAL TIPS

If you're lucky, the Judoon (see page 52) will catch a Plasmavore before it gets you. Florence had Slabs – like bikers in leather – helping her. In fact, the Slabs were MADE of leather. If you have an X-ray machine handy, the radiation can destroy the Slabs.

Disguised as a granny called Florence.

Sucks blood from her victims using a bendy straw. Well, that's original, I suppose.

Can change its internal biology to match its victim's.

MONSTER DATA

ORIGIN

UNKNOWN

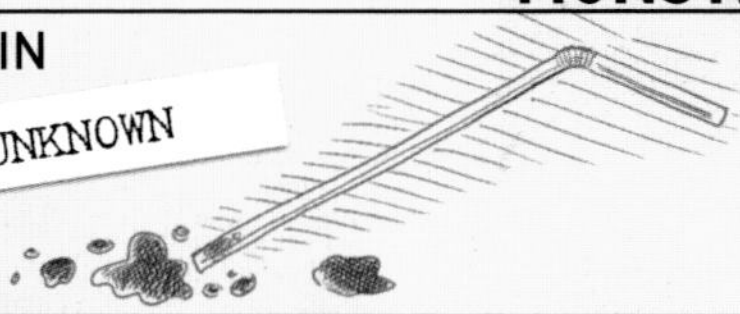

SPEED

SLOW – FAST

0 1 2 3 4 5 6 7 8 9 10 (5 circled)

DANGEROUS RATING

SAFE – DEADLY

0 1 2 3 4 5 6 7 8 9 10 (6 circled)

SIZE

 # JUDOON

IMAGINE A RHINO IN A SPACESUIT.
Got it? That's a Judoon. Special
helmet, obviously, that sticks out
at the front, so there's room for
the horns and stuff. The Judoon
are like a police force for hire.
Other races employ them to bring
criminals to justice. Judoon
justice is very swift and
quite brutal.

See, I told you: rhino in a spacesuit.

They've got a tough hide, but their
space armour is even tougher.

Various tools for scanning, translation,
and other useful stuff. I expect.

Judoon aren't allowed on Earth. So they cheat. They use an H_2O scoop, which transports people or even buildings somewhere else. Like the Moon. It creates quite a storm, a real storm, with lightning and everything, except - and this is really weird - the rain falls *upwards* instead of down.

SURVIVAL TIPS

Great stampy, noisy, shouty things - you can hear the Judoon coming a mile off. Then things get broken. So be on your best behaviour. Answering back can get you locked up. Fighting back gets you executed. So it's like being at school, only worse. If you can imagine that.

MONSTER DATA

ORIGIN

UNKNOWN

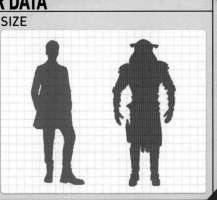

SIZE

SPEED

SLOW — FAST
0 1 2 3 4 5 6 7 8 9 10

DANGEROUS RATING

SAFE — DEADLY
0 1 2 3 4 5 6 7 8 9 10

SPOONHEADS

WALKING WI-FI BASE STATIONS, SPOONHEADS DUMP PEOPLE INTO DIGITAL STORAGE. They look sort of like people - except for the scooped-out back of the head. Pretty basic robots with heads like the back of a spoon.

SURVIVAL TIPS

Spoonheads often copy people who exist in your mind but not in the real world, such as characters in books you've read. If you're any good at hacking computers, this could be your big chance.

Looks human from the front.

Not so human from the back — more spoon-y.

Actually a robotic computer server ready to suck out your brain.

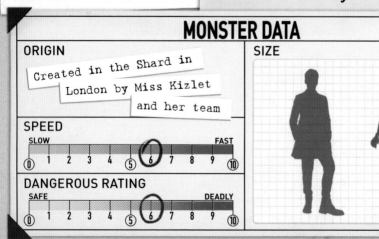

MONSTER DATA

ORIGIN

Created in the Shard in London by Miss Kizlet and her team

SIZE

SPEED

SLOW										FAST
⓪	1	2	3	4	⑤	6	7	8	9	⑩

DANGEROUS RATING

SAFE										DEADLY
⓪	1	2	3	4	⑤	6	7	8	9	⑩

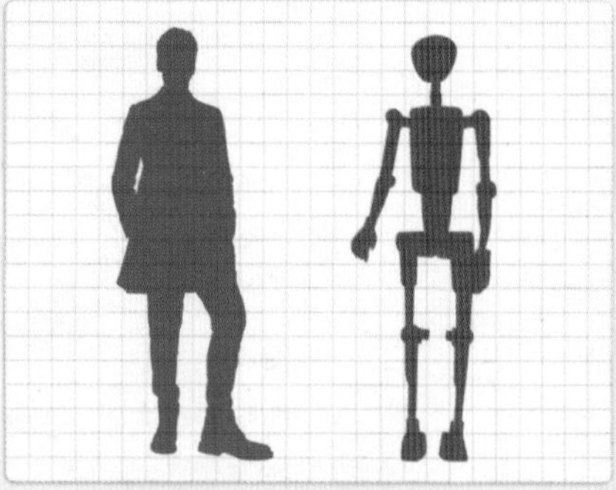

LAZARUS CREATURE

PROFESSOR RICHARD LAZARUS TRIED TO BECOME YOUNG AGAIN USING A GENETIC MANIPULATION DEVICE. Good news: he succeeded. Bad news: it messed up his DNA, and he turned into a primordial arthropod creature. So not really a very successful experiment, after all.

Human face just about visible. And just about human.

Exoskeleton. In other words, he's bony on the outside.

Deadly sting in the tail.

Sharp, spiky limbs.

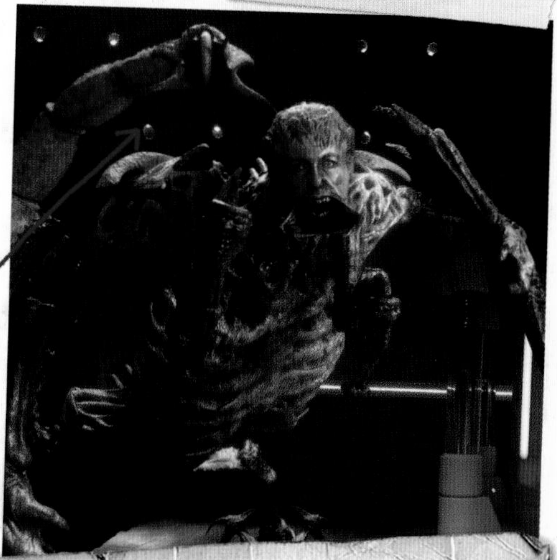

SURVIVAL TIPS

Well, he's easy to spot, I suppose. Rather stands out at a posh reception where there's nibbles and drinks and you're expecting to celebrate a scientific breakthrough. Best option – play extremely loud music to disrupt

MONSTER DATA

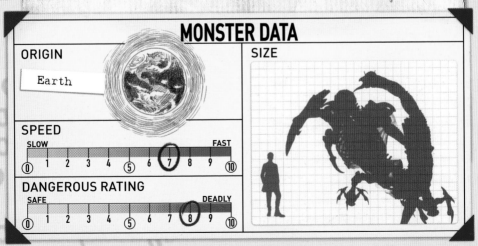

ORIGIN

Earth

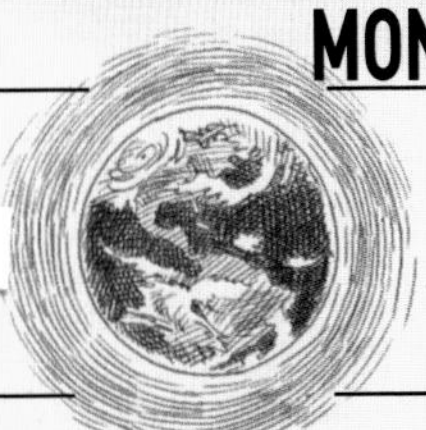

SIZE

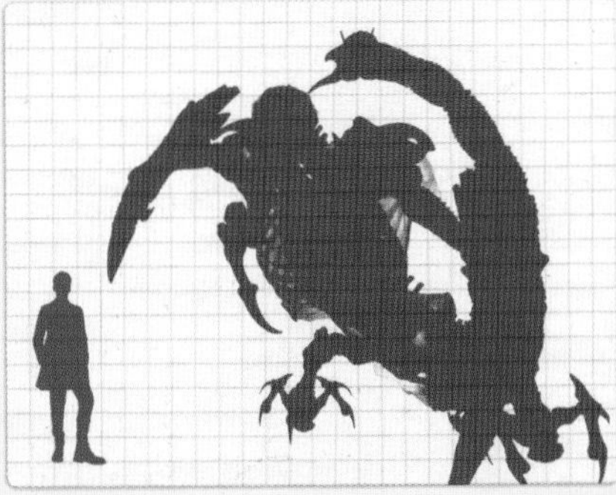

SPEED

SLOW 0 1 2 3 4 5 6 7 8 9 10 FAST (7 circled)

DANGEROUS RATING

SAFE 0 1 2 3 4 5 6 7 8 9 10 DEADLY (8 circled)

THE BONELESS

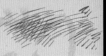

THAT'S WHAT I CALLED THEM, ANYWAY. Creatures from another plane of existence where everything was completely flat. Which was fine - until they started flattening people. They trapped me inside a shrinking TARDIS, too, and that was never going to win them any favours.

The Boneless were completely flat in our world.

Gradually, they managed to manipulate the dimensions here.

Then they shrank the TARDIS. With me inside! That's just not on, you know.

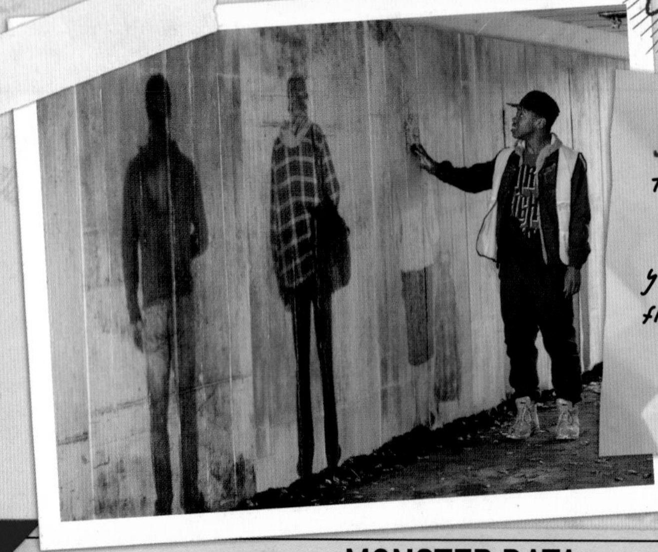

SURVIVAL TIPS

There's no way of telling the Boneless are there, unless you see someone that's been flattened. The only thing you can do is make sure they don't touch you.

MONSTER DATA

ORIGIN

Some other, two-dimensional plane of existence

SPEED

SLOW 0 1 2 3 4 5 6 7 [8] 9 10 FAST

DANGEROUS RATING

SAFE 0 1 2 3 4 5 6 7 [8] 9 10 DEADLY

SIZE

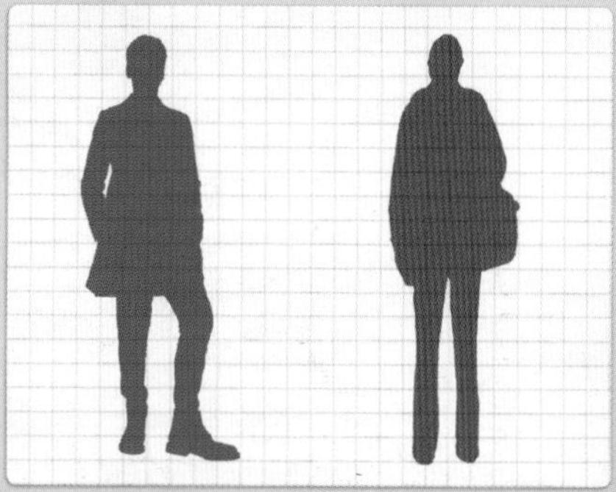

GIANT SPIDERS

SPIDERS, ONLY HUGE. In fact one called the Great One, as the not very original name suggests, was *enormously* huge. The spiders lived on Metebelis 3, and were enlarged and mutated by the powers of the strange blue crystals there. But then the spiders managed to find a way to Earth . . .

Legs. Eight of them. Obviously.

Devours humans for lunch.

Also shoots deadly energy.

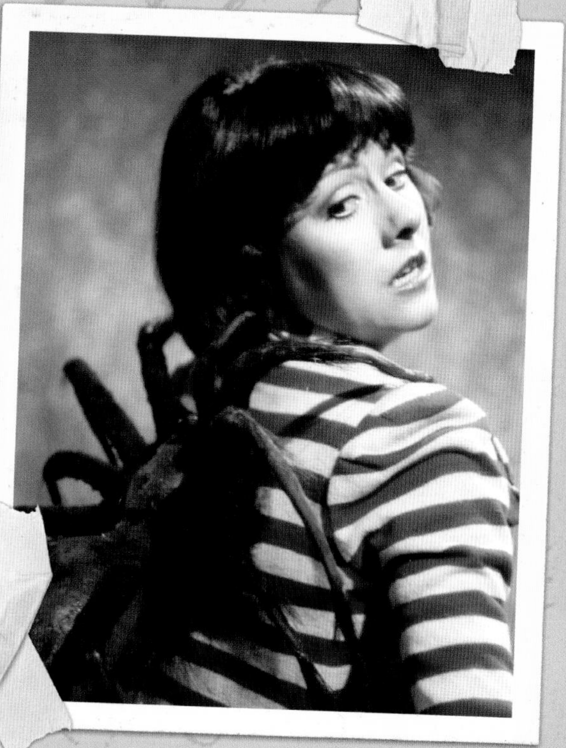

SURVIVAL TIPS

I'm assuming you'd notice a big spider scuttling about or waiting for you in the bath. Keep well back as they can jump. If one lands on you, it can clamp on to your back and control your mind.

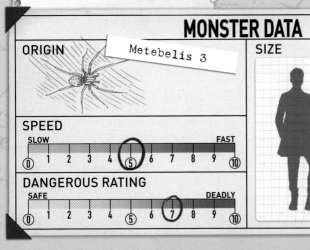

MONSTER DATA

ORIGIN

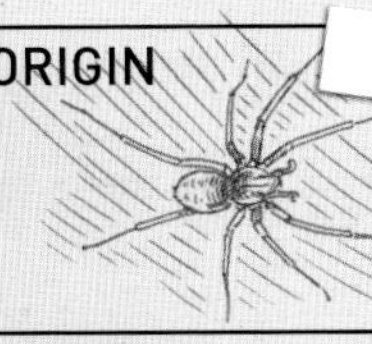

Metebelis 3

SIZE

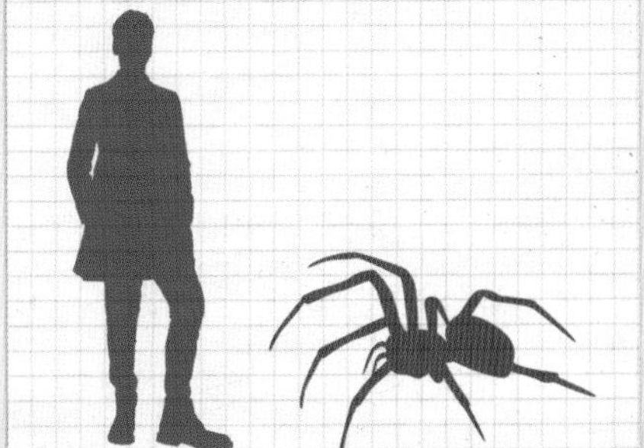

SPEED

SLOW — FAST

0 1 2 3 4 (5) 6 7 8 9 10

DANGEROUS RATING

SAFE — DEADLY

0 1 2 3 4 5 6 (7) 8 9 10

SPIDER GERMS

THESE LOOK LIKE SPIDERS - EVEN BIGGER THAN THE
SPIDERS ON METEBELIS 3 - BUT ACTUALLY THEY'RE
GERMS. They were living on the Moon, which was really a
giant egg. Is this making any sense? Anyway - big, horrid,
hairy spider germs.

Spider - body,
legs, the usual -
but deadly.

Beady little
red eyes. Hope
they don't
see you.

They move
pretty quickly,
so be careful.

SURVIVAL TIPS

Unless you're on the Moon, you should be all right.
Otherwise, try detergent spray or sunlight. Or whack
them with a large hammer, but that could get squishy.

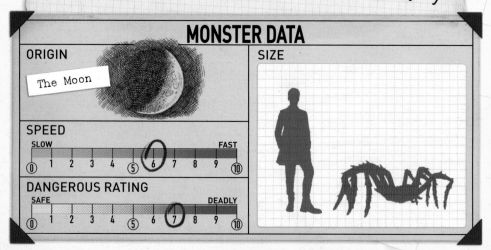

MONSTER DATA

ORIGIN

The Moon

SPEED

SLOW · 0 1 2 3 4 5 ⑥ 7 8 9 10 · FAST

DANGEROUS RATING

SAFE · 0 1 2 3 4 5 6 ⑦ 8 9 10 · DEADLY

SIZE

 # RACNOSS

GIGANTIC SPIDERY CREATURES FROM THE ANCIENT DARK TIMES. Born starving, they'd eat anything, even planets. Luckily, the Racnoss were wiped out by the Fledgling Empires. Not so luckily, the Empress of the Racnoss survived in hibernation on her Webstar. When she woke up she went looking for the eggs she'd laid, and guess what? Planet Earth had formed round them. Not good.

Eyes. Lots of eyes.

Legs. Lots of legs. And they end in points, like spears.

SURVIVAL TIPS

The good news is that I sorted the Empress out, with a bit of help from Donna Noble. I also flushed her children down the plughole. Big plughole. So, unless there are more Racnoss eggs somewhere, you should be all right. But watch out for exploding killer Christmas trees or for Santa Claus behaving strangely . . .

Huge, bulbous, spider-like body.

Ability to teleport.

MONSTER DATA

ORIGIN

The Dark Times - billions of years ago

SIZE

SPEED

SLOW | 0 1 2 3 4 5 **6** 7 8 9 10 | FAST

DANGEROUS RATING

SAFE | 0 1 2 3 4 5 6 7 **8** 9 10 | DEADLY

STINGRAYS

THESE ARE NOT REALLY STINGRAYS, THEY JUST LOOK A BIT LIKE THEM. Difference is, these fly, and swarm in their billions; they also devastate whole planets, eating everything in their path. They fly so fast they create a wormhole to take them to their next meal: another planet.

Big mouth with lots of teeth. Sharp teeth.

They even eat metal, and turn it into their bones – so their skeleton is made of METAL.

SURVIVAL TIPS

If these things arrive on your planet, sorry, but you've had it – they'll leave it a desert. Unless the Unified Intelligence Taskforce is there to shoot them down. Make sure you have UNIT on speed-dial.

Dangerous sharp tail.

MONSTER DATA

ORIGIN

Unknown

SPEED

SLOW — FAST

0 1 2 3 4 (5) 6 7 8 9 (10)

DANGEROUS RATING

SAFE — DEADLY

0 1 2 3 4 (5) 6 7 (8) 9 10

SIZE

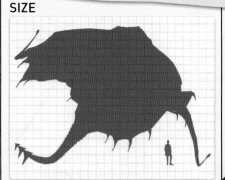

TRITOVORES

TRITOVORES LOOK LIKE NASTY GIANT FLIES, BUT ACTUALLY THEY'RE FRIENDLY ENOUGH. You just might not want them round for dinner, not least because you wouldn't understand what they were saying - though they'll understand you all right, which isn't really fair if you ask me.

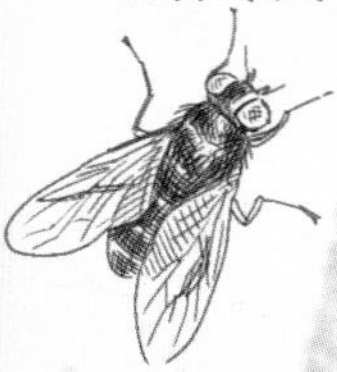

Bristly dark hair.
Big multifaceted eyes.
Mandibles.
Basically, it's a fly in space overalls.

SURVIVAL TIPS

You probably won't meet any Tritovores, as they're from the Scorpion Nebula, which is a long, long way away. So why am I wasting my time telling you all this?

MONSTER DATA

ORIGIN

The Scorpion Nebula

SPEED

SLOW 0 1 2 3 4 5 (6) 7 8 9 10 FAST

DANGEROUS RATING

SAFE 0 1 (2) 3 4 5 6 7 8 9 10 DEADLY

SIZE

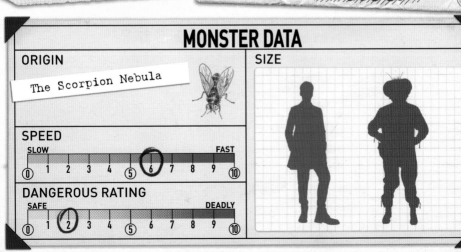

CATKIND

BIG, TALL, HUMANOID CATS WHO LIVED ON NEW EARTH. I have to say, not all Catkind are bad any more than all humans are bad - though you do sometimes wonder. But the Sisters of Plenitude, who ran a big hospital, weren't the best. Their idea of medical research was highly dubious.

Looks like a cat, only bigger. And standing on two feet.

Let's face it, this IS a cat.

With whiskers and everything.

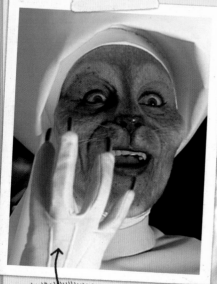

'And everything' includes razor-sharp claws.

The Sisters of Plenitude created specially grown humans who they kept comatose in the 'Intensive Care Unit' of their hospital. The Sisters infected the humans with every known disease, making them incubators for the cures the Sisters needed. There are good ways of developing new medicines, but this isn't one of them.

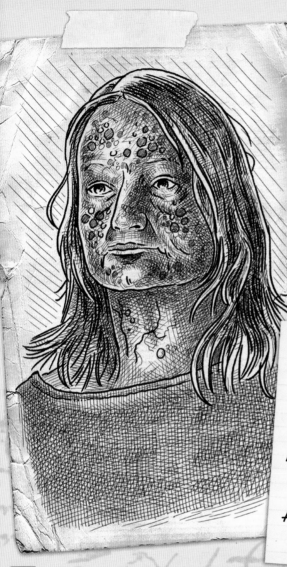

SURVIVAL TIPS

Like I said, not all Catkind are bad. I met a few friendly Catkind. But, if a big cat dressed like a nun tries to put you inside a suspended-animation booth and infect you with every known disease, you've found one of the bad ones. You'll need a mixture of all known medicines to survive.

MONSTER DATA

ORIGIN
New Earth

SIZE

SPEED
SLOW — FAST
0 1 2 3 4 (5) 6 7 8 9 10

DANGEROUS RATING
SAFE — DEADLY
0 1 2 3 4 (5) 6 7 8 9 10

KRILLITANES

Leathery skin.

Sharp claws.

Bat-like features inherited (that means stolen) from the inhabitants of Bessan.

And they can fly. Of course they can fly – I mean, look at those wings.

THE KRILLITANES ARE A MIXTURE OF OTHER SPECIES - THEY ABSORB THE CHARACTERISTICS OF THE RACES THEY CONQUER, WHICH IS BOTH CLEVER AND RARE. When I met them, they were like giant orange bats, but they were pretending to be school teachers - there's some similarity between the two, I suppose. The Krillitanes want to control and rule the universe, and that's never a good start.

The Krillitanes I met used clever school kids to crack the Skasis Paradigm - that's the key to how the universe works. Once they'd figured that out, the Krillitanes thought they could control, well, everything everywhere ever. Fortunately I stopped them before they got to find out if they actually could have.

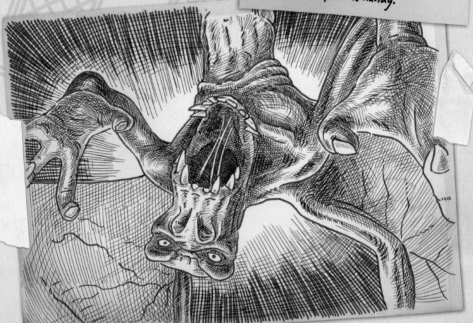

MONSTER DATA

ORIGIN

Unknown

SPEED

SLOW										FAST
⓪	1	2	3	4	⑤	6	7	8	⑨	10

DANGEROUS RATING

SAFE										DEADLY
⓪	1	2	3	4	⑤	6	7	⑧	9	10

SIZE

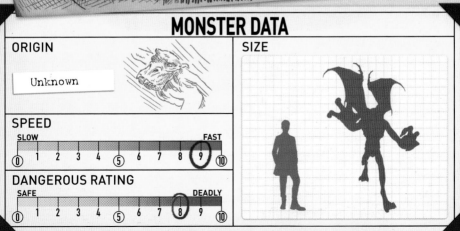

MIDNIGHT ENTITY

ON A PLANET MADE OF DIAMOND, I ENCOUNTERED
A CREATURE THAT STOLE MY VOICE. It nearly stole my
thoughts, too. I've no idea what it really looked like,
or what it was. I just hope I never meet it again . . .

First it takes
your voice.

It repeats what
you say. Then it says
it with you. Then
BEFORE you.

Then it steals
your thoughts –
your mind.

SURVIVAL TIPS

It's not often that something really scares me. But the
creature on Midnight did. I have no idea how you can escape
from it – apart from not visiting the planet Midnight.

MONSTER DATA

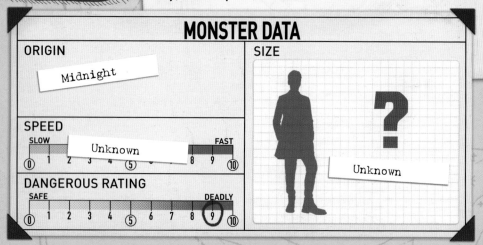

ORIGIN

Midnight

SPEED

SLOW   FAST
0   1   2   3   4   5   6   7   8   9   10

Unknown

DANGEROUS RATING

SAFE   DEADLY
0   1   2   3   4   5   6   7   8   9   10

SIZE

?

Unknown

KRAFAYIS

KRAFAYIS ARE SAVAGE HUNTERS AND SCAVENGERS. They're also invisible to most people. Only person I met who could see a Krafayis was the painter Vincent van Gogh - but he saw the whole world in a very different way from most people.

Most people can't see a Krafayis.

Not unless they're incredibly gifted.

Or incredibly clever and can rig up a device like this. Neat, eh?

SURVIVAL TIPS

You won't see a Krafayis coming, but you'll know where it's been. You'll need to find someone lucky (or unlucky) enough to be able to see the creature for you so that you can keep well clear.

MONSTER DATA

ORIGIN Some say the Krafayis originated on Gallifrey - they certainly appear in Time Lord legends

SPEED

SLOW 0 1 2 3 4 ⑤ 6 7 ⑧ 9 ⑩ FAST

DANGEROUS RATING

SAFE 0 1 2 3 4 ⑤ 6 7 ⑧ 9 ⑩ DEADLY

SIZE

?

Hard to tell - they're invisible

VESPIFORM

THE VESPIFORM ARE A WISE AND ANCIENT RACE THAT
LOOK LIKE GIANT WASPS. Well, nobody's perfect. But
they can change their appearance; when they do,
they store their mind in a telepathic recorder.
They've got a vicious sting on them.

Big wasp. Big. Really - big!

Keep out of the way of the killer sting.

Vespiforms grow their massive stingers back after use.

SURVIVAL TIPS

Listen for loud buzzing. Watch out for huge wasps. At that size, a rolled-up newspaper isn't going to work. But chuck its telepathic recorder into a lake, and it might drown trying to retrieve it.

MONSTER DATA

ORIGIN

Hives in the Silfrax Galaxy

SIZE

SPEED

SLOW | FAST
0 1 2 3 4 5 6 7 ⑧ 9 10

DANGEROUS RATING

SAFE | DEADLY
0 1 2 3 4 5 6 ⑦ 8 9 10

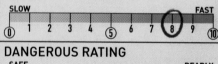

MACRA

COLOSSAL CRUSTACEANS, A BIT LIKE GIANT CRABS. The Macra depend on a toxic gas to survive - they ingest it like food. On one human colony I visited, they'd brainwashed the people there into mining the gas for them.

SURVIVAL TIPS

Macra don't like bright lights, and they need their gas to survive. So stop their gas supply any way you can and keep a powerful torch to hand.

It's a giant crab creature.

Eyes out on stalks – and they can see in the dark.

Huge pincers and claws.

MONSTER DATA

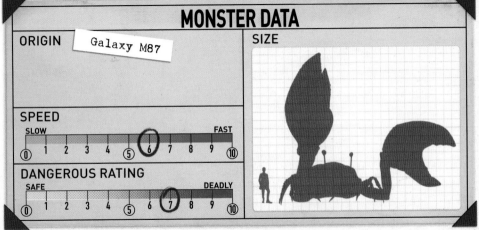

ORIGIN: Galaxy M87

SIZE

SPEED

SLOW										FAST
0	1	2	3	4	5	6	7	8	9	10

DANGEROUS RATING

SAFE										DEADLY
0	1	2	3	4	5	6	7	8	9	10

WINDERS AND SMILERS

DON'T BE FOOLED BY THEIR FROZEN SMILES - these security and information androids from the *Starship UK* have quick tempers and heads that spin round and snarl when you disobey or anger them.

Smiler - sits in an information or teaching booth. Mostly.

Rotating heads reveal their dark sides.

Winder - more mobile and therefore more dangerous.

SURVIVAL TIPS

Don't mention the Star Whale. Seriously – not a word. Just shut it, all right? Oh, and do well at school. Forget detention – the Smiler teacher will simply feed you straight to the Star Whale as a snack. And you probably don't want that.

The Smilers and Winders wanted to protect the great secret of *Starship UK* at all costs. The great secret was that the spaceship was being carried by a huge Star Whale – the humans were forcing it to carry them, but in fact, once freed, it was happy to help anyway.

MONSTER DATA

ORIGIN Starship UK

SPEED Smilers

SLOW ⓪ ① 2 3 4 ⑤ 6 7 8 9 ⑩ FAST

Winders

SLOW ⓪ 1 2 3 4 ⑤ ⑥ 7 8 9 ⑩ FAST

DANGEROUS RATING

SAFE ⓪ 1 2 3 ④ ⑤ 6 7 8 9 ⑩ DEADLY

SIZE

Winder

Smiler

CYBERMEN

SURVIVAL: THE BASIC
INSTINCT OF ANY RACE.
The Cybermen took it to the
extreme. They replaced their
bodies with metal and plastic,
becoming machines. And then -
as if that wasn't enough
- they messed with their
brains too, removing all
emotion and feeling.
They thought it was an
improvement. It wasn't.

Rods connect
directly to the
brain, or what's
left of it.

Cybermen want to survive,
at any cost. They'll
turn everyone else into
Cybermen to do it.

People without
emotions, made
from metal
and plastic.

Everything is enhanced
and stronger - eyes,
limbs, everything.

The Cybermen constantly upgrade themselves, finding ways to become stronger and more efficient. Completely daft - if they just thought about it a bit, they'd realise that there's no substitute for feelings. They can't replace what they've lost with logic and computers. They're very strong, very clever idiots.

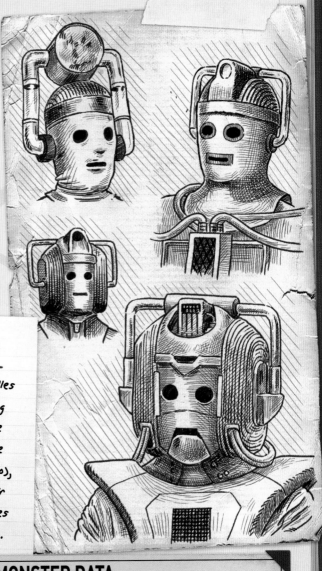

SURVIVAL TIPS

Shadows of big figures with handles on their heads and loud stomping noises are clues that there are Cybermen about. They don't like radiation (but that'll kill you too), or solvents (which dissolve their plastic bits). Gold dust sometimes works, if you have some handy ...

MONSTER DATA

ORIGIN	SIZE
Mondas, the twin planet of Earth	
Also, a parallel version of Earth	

SPEED

SLOW   FAST

⓪ 1 2 3 4 ⑤ 6 **7** 8 9 ⑩

DANGEROUS RATING

SAFE   DEADLY

⓪ 1 2 3 4 ⑤ 6 7 8 **9** ⑩

CYBER CONTROLLER

THE BIG BOSS CYBERMAN IS CALLED THE CONTROLLER. There have been a few - probably because someone (guess who) keeps destroying them. Like Cybermen, the design develops. But the Controller always has an enlarged brain case on top of its head - for its enlarged brain. Still no feelings or emotions though, so it's a pretty rubbish brain no matter how whopping it is.

Tubes connect the Cyber Controller to the main network systems.

Brain visible through transparent head case.

'Head case' is about right. Unfeeling, cold, deadly . . .

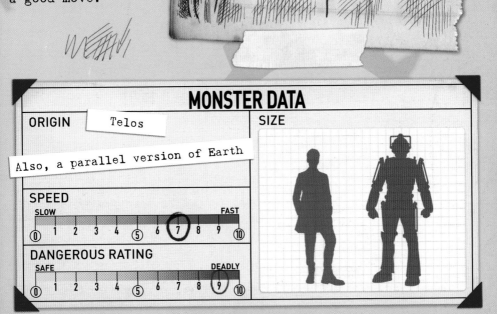

SURVIVAL TIPS

Same advice as for ordinary Cybermen. But if the Controller's around, there are likely to be loads of other Cybermen nearby, too. Not only that, but the Controller's even stronger and bigger and more powerful than other Cybermen. You can try electrocuting him - plug in and hope (that's something else the Cybermen can't do).

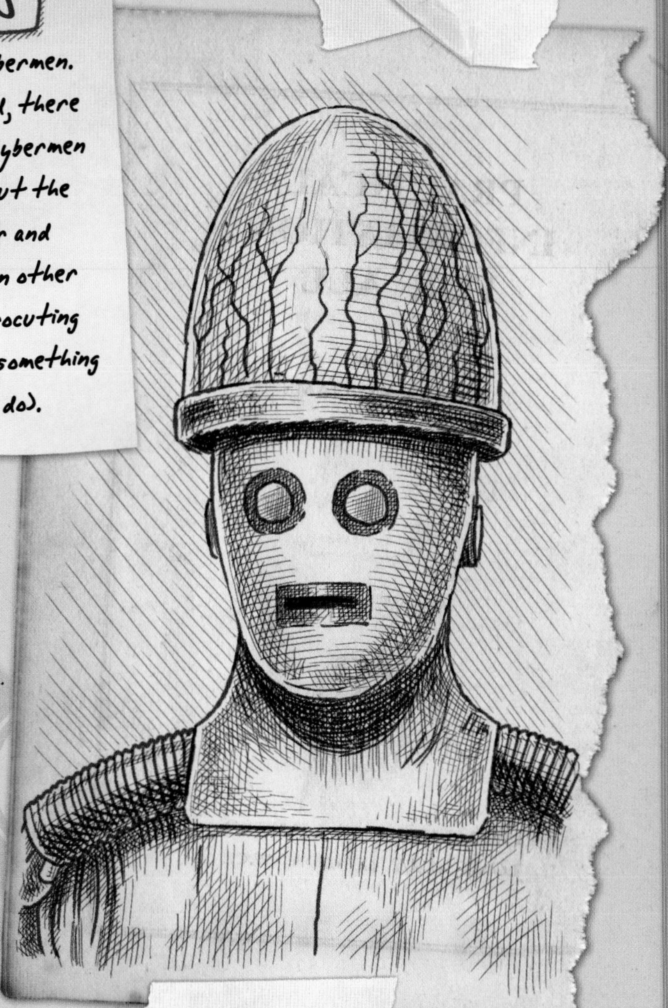

The first Cyber Controller I met was on planet Telos. The Cybermen were hibernating (or whatever Cybermen do) in ice tombs deep beneath their city. And some fool woke them up. Never a good move.

MONSTER DATA

ORIGIN   Telos

Also, a parallel version of Earth

SIZE

SPEED

SLOW   FAST

⓪ 1 2 3 4 ⑤ 6 ⑦ 8 9 ⑩

DANGEROUS RATING

SAFE   DEADLY

⓪ 1 2 3 4 ⑤ 6 7 8 ⑨ ⑩

CYBERSHADES

WHEN A GROUP OF CYBERMEN GOT STRANDED IN VICTORIAN LONDON, THEY CREATED CYBERSHADES - creatures made from whatever animals the Cybermen could find, upgraded (they thought!) with whatever technology they could find or adapt.

Furry, but definitely not to be kept as a pet. Unless you're a Cyberman.

Could climb walls and run fast on all fours.

Hands and head upgraded with available Victorian materials.

SURVIVAL TIPS

Thankfully, Cybershades are only found in Victorian London. But keep an eye out anyway. Any missing dogs or cats or even badgers could be a clue that there are Cybermen experimenting and plotting an attack . . .

MONSTER DATA

ORIGIN

Victorian London in 1851

SPEED

SLOW 0 1 2 3 4 5 6 7 8 9 10 FAST

DANGEROUS RATING

SAFE 0 1 2 3 4 5 6 7 8 9 10 DEADLY

SIZE

CYBERKING

THE SO-CALLED CYBERKING WAS ACTUALLY A DREADNOUGHT-CLASS CYBER SHIP. It might have looked like a mammoth, industrial-style Cyberman, but, actually, the main body contained a Cyber Factory ready to convert millions of humans into Cybermen.

A power-mad human called Miss Hartigan was converted into the CyberKing.

It stomped all over London.

Built-in weaponry in the arms meant no one was safe.

SURVIVAL TIPS

Well, keep out of its way, obviously. You don't want to get squashed or blasted. If you're a complete genius, then you could go up in a hot-air balloon and destroy it. Just an idea.

MONSTER DATA

ORIGIN

Victorian London in 1851

SIZE

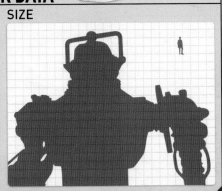

SPEED

SLOW   FAST

0 1 2 3 4 5 6 7 **8** 9 10

DANGEROUS RATING

SAFE   DEADLY

0 1 2 3 4 5 6 7 8 **9** 10

CYBERMATS

CYBERMATS ARE LIKE METAL, CYBERNETIC RODENTS. They probably were rodents once. They're programmed to perform simple tasks, and they can scuttle about in places where a Cyberman might be noticed or won't fit.

WATCH OUT – THEY BITE.

They can drain electrical energy.

They can home in on your brainwaves.

Like the Cybermen themselves, the Cybermats have evolved and changed over time. They are adapted according to whatever task the Cybermen want them to perform - spreading a deadly plague, destroying fuel stocks, or just plain killing people,. . .

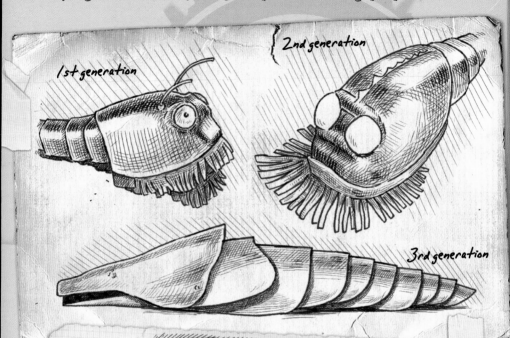

1st generation

2nd generation

3rd generation

SURVIVAL TIPS

Tell-tale signs that there are Cybermats about include: scratches on the floor, destroyed Bernalium rods, a deadly plague that suddenly spreads with no explanation, dead people and Cybermen, obviously. Your best bet is to confuse them with electrical energy.

MONSTER DATA

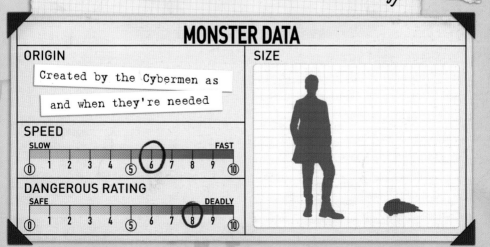

ORIGIN

Created by the Cybermen as and when they're needed

SPEED

SLOW — FAST
0 1 2 3 4 (5) 6 7 8 9 (10)

DANGEROUS RATING

SAFE — DEADLY
0 1 2 3 4 (5) 6 7 8 9 (10)

SIZE

CYBER-DOCTOR

I GOT PARTIALLY CONVERTED INTO A CYBERMAN ONCE. Not fun. I had to go inside my own mind and talk myself out of it. Not many people could do that. Well, probably no one - except me. Lucky I was there, really.

Cybernetic appendages.

I was attacked by Cybermites (we'll get to them next).

IT HURT A LOT.

SURVIVAL TIPS

It was like I was two people at once — Real-Me and Cyber-Me. I'm hoping it won't happen again. But, if it does, make sure you're talking to Real-Me before you do what I tell you.

MONSTER DATA

ORIGIN

This was at Hedgewick's World of Wonders.

A fun day out - not

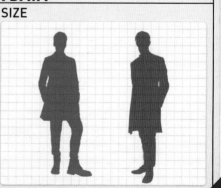

SIZE

SPEED

SLOW										FAST
0	1	2	3	4	5	6	7	8	9	10

DANGEROUS RATING

SAFE										DEADLY
0	1	2	3	4	5	6	7	8	9	10

CYBERMITES

LIKE CYBERMATS, ONLY SMALLER. Tiny, in fact. Cybermites seek out potential material and convert it into Cybermen. And that potential material is people - like you and me. Really like me, in fact, as I found out at Hedgewick's World.

Little tiny wee cybernetic beasties.

Small is still dangerous.

SURVIVAL TIPS

Once Cybermites get you, you're in trouble. If anyone suddenly has metal bits growing out of their hands or face - or anywhere else - then watch out for Cybermites. And Cybermen.

MONSTER DATA

ORIGIN

Wherever there are Cybermen

SPEED

SLOW | | | | | | | | | | FAST
(0) 1 2 3 4 (5) 6 7 8 9 (10)

DANGEROUS RATING

SAFE | | | | | | | | | | DEADLY
(0) 1 2 3 4 (5) 6 (7) 8 9 (10)

SIZE

3W CYBERMEN

THE 3W INSTITUTE CREATED A WHOLE CITY FOR DEAD PEOPLE. All an illusion. Oh, you might wake up one day dead (so you won't have actually woken up at all) and find yourself there. But you're not really. You - are - dead. 3W was storing the minds of dead people, ready to download into dead bodies - dead bodies that were then upgraded into Cybermen.

When submerged in 'dark water', the Cybermen appeared as skeletons.

But they're Cybermen - dangerous and deadly . . .

That's because, inside each Cyberman, that's what there is - a skeleton.

Every tiny particle of a Cyberman contains the plans to make another Cyberman. If it makes contact with suitable organic material – *WALLOP!* another Cyberman. And suitable organic material might be dead bodies. In a graveyard. A graveyard where it's raining Cyber-pollen.

MONSTER DATA

ORIGIN

Dead people. Unpleasant, but there it is

SPEED

SLOW 0 1 2 3 4 5 6 7 8 9 10 FAST

DANGEROUS RATING

SAFE 0 1 2 3 4 5 6 7 8 9 10 DEADLY

SIZE

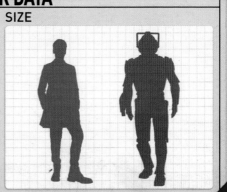

NESTENE CONSCIOUSNESS

WHAT KIND OF DAFT MONSTER DOESN'T EVEN HAVE A SHAPE? The Nestene Consciousness, that's what. It has to make itself a body. Out of plastic. And it can control other things made of plastic, too, which I suppose is a bit more clever - and quite scary.

Its shape keeps changing - while making ugly faces at you, which isn't very nice.

Usually it's a great gloop of gunky plastic soup. Probably tastes disgusting.

Can transfer its intelligence to other plastic objects.

Makes its own body.

SURVIVAL TIPS

If you're stupid enough to be around when plastic stuff comes to life, there's not a lot you can do. Just don't be so mindless as to hide behind a plastic sofa – that will never end well. Anti-plastic is the best stuff to use against the Nestenes, so keep some around for emergencies.

The first time I met the Nestene Consciousness it grew itself a rather unpleasant octopus-like form. Lots of tentacles. I hate tentacles – all those suckers, and always trying to hug you. What is it with other life forms and hugging?

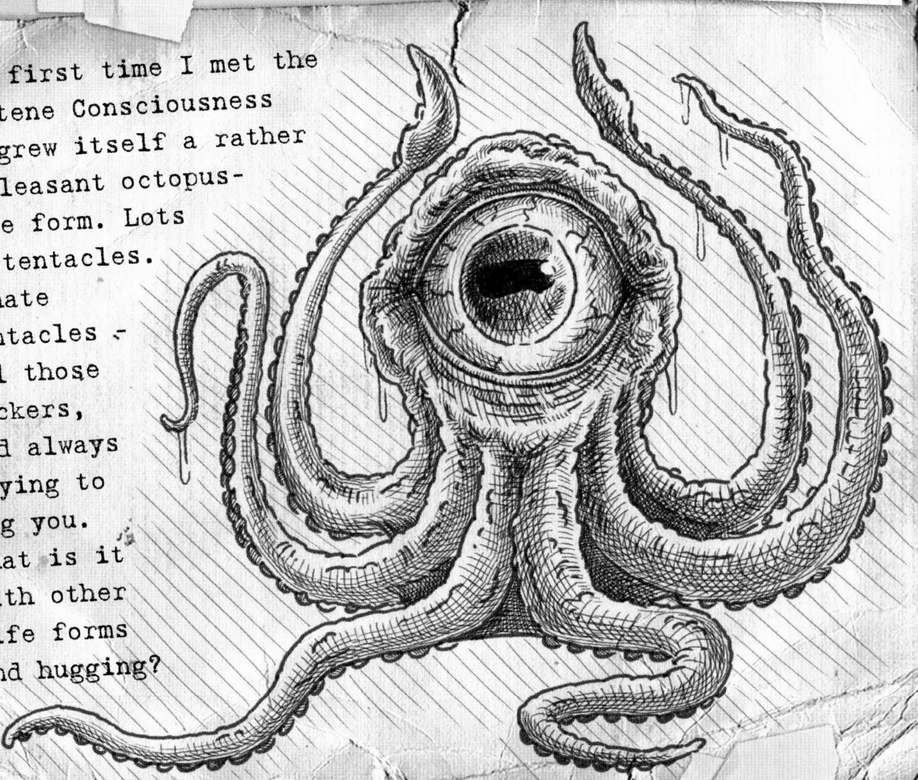

MONSTER DATA

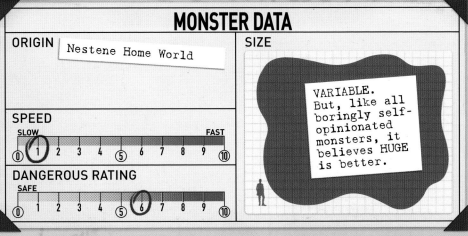

ORIGIN

Nestene Home World

SIZE

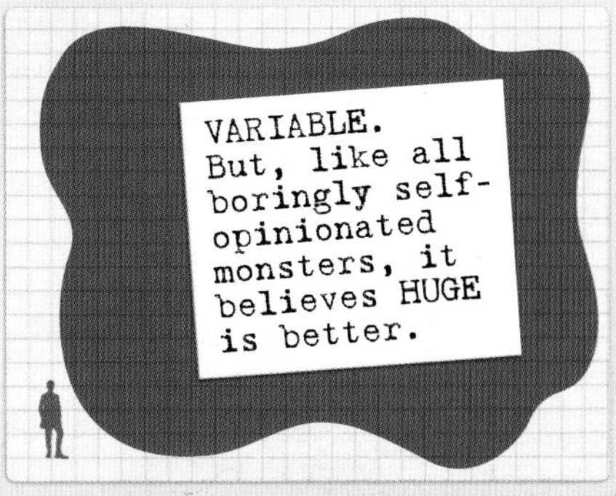
VARIABLE.
But, like all boringly self-opinionated monsters, it believes HUGE is better.

SPEED

SLOW 0 1 2 3 4 5 6 7 8 9 10 FAST (1 circled)

DANGEROUS RATING

SAFE 0 1 2 3 4 5 6 7 8 9 10 (6 circled)

AUTONS

REMEMBER WHAT I SAID ABOUT THE NESTENE CONSCIOUSNESS BEING ABLE TO BRING PLASTIC THINGS TO LIFE? Course you do - it was only a page ago. Well, one thing it likes to bring to life is plastic shop-window dummies. With guns hidden in their wrists. They're called Autons, and they are scary and dangerous.

A shop-window dummy. But alive.

Fashion sense depends on what shop it came from.

Gun hidden in wrist.

SURVIVAL TIPS

If shop dummies start moving, then run. Keep an eye on anyone important, too – like teachers or traffic wardens. If they're acting strangely and look plasticky, they might be Nestene duplicates. If their hand drops down and a gun pops out, it's a certainty: you need to find and stop the Nestene Consciousness.

Not just dummies. The Autons walk and kill, and that's about it. But Nestenes can also create exact duplicates of people. They look a bit shiny and, well, plasticky, to be honest. But they fool most people.

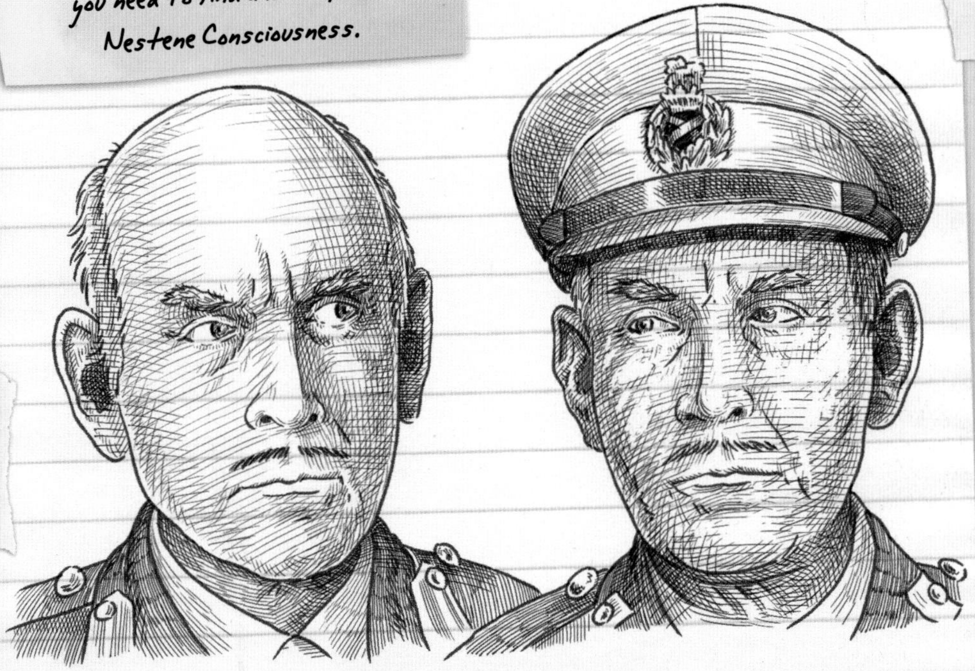

MONSTER DATA

ORIGIN

Animated by the Nestene Consciousness

SIZE

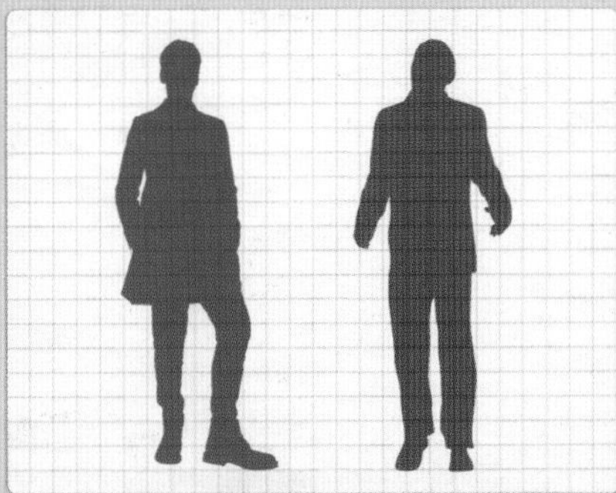

SPEED

SLOW – FAST: 0 1 2 3 4 5 6 [7] 8 9 10

DANGEROUS RATING

SAFE – DEADLY: 0 1 2 3 4 5 6 7 [8] 9 10

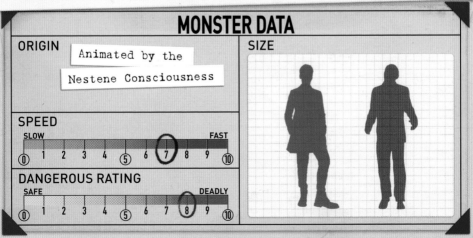

CASSANDRA

HEARD THE EXPRESSION 'NOT JUST A PRETTY FACE'? Well, Lady Cassandra O'Brien Dot Delta Seventeen - to give her (very) full name - was just a pretty face. Stretched over a metal frame. Devious, opinionated, vain and ambitious. A shopping trolley with attitude.

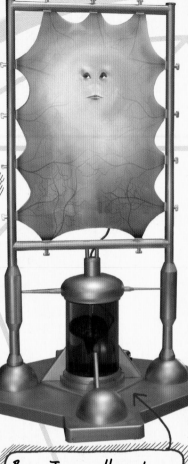

Face is skin stretched over a frame.

Cassandra had any wrinkles cut out. What's she got against wrinkles? They make you look distinguished.

SURVIVAL TIPS

You'll soon know when Cassandra is around. On and on she goes about how beautiful she is. And how thin. Best way to shut her up is to dry her out - without moisturising, her skin dries, shrinks, and snaps. Twang. End of.

Brain. In a jar. Honestly.

MONSTER DATA

ORIGIN Earth. Or so she said, but really - I mean, look at her! Last 'pure human'? I don't think so

SIZE

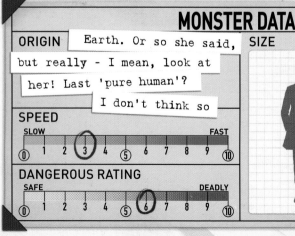

SPEED

SLOW   FAST
⓪ 1 2 ③ 4 ⑤ 6 7 8 9 ⑩

DANGEROUS RATING

SAFE   DEADLY
⓪ 1 2 3 4 ⑤ ⑥ 7 8 9 ⑩

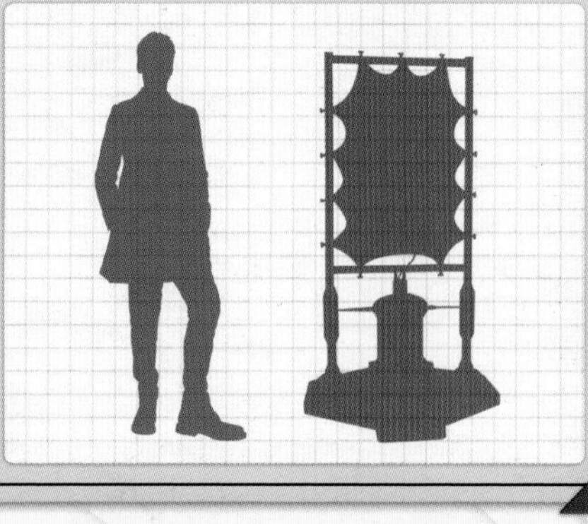

ROBOT SPIDERS

THEY'RE NOT REALLY SPIDERS. They only have four legs. And they're metal. And robots. Cassandra used them to sabotage Platform One. They got inside the systems, and it was up to yours truly to save the day. As usual.

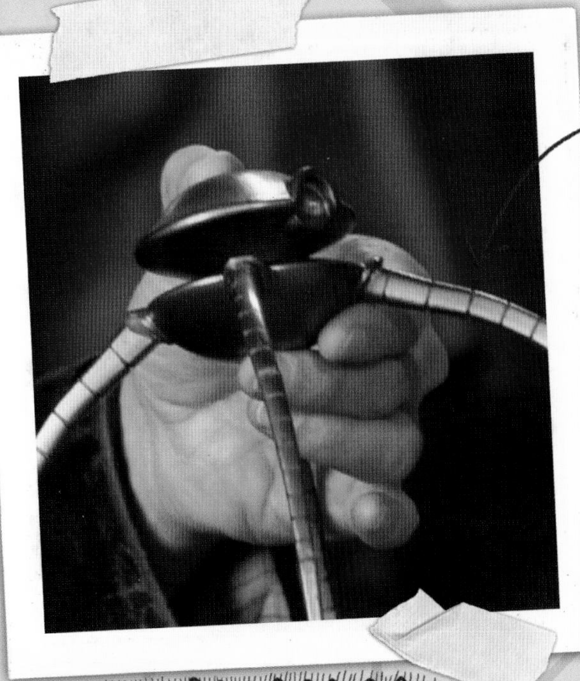

Segmented metal legs. Four of them (so, like I said, not really a spider).

Eye can fire a light or laser beam.

Oh, and they can explode too.

SURVIVAL TIPS

If your systems go wrong, these little creatures could be to blame. One of them's not much trouble – apart from its laser-beam eye. But when there are dozens you should worry.

MONSTER DATA

ORIGIN

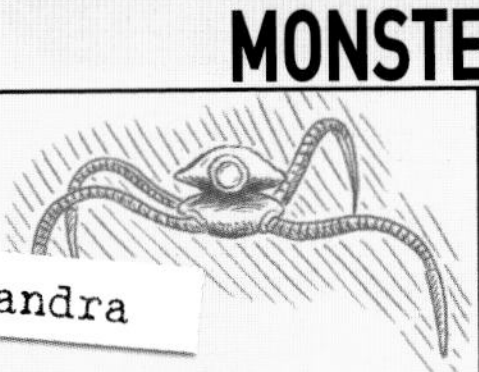

Created by Cassandra

SIZE

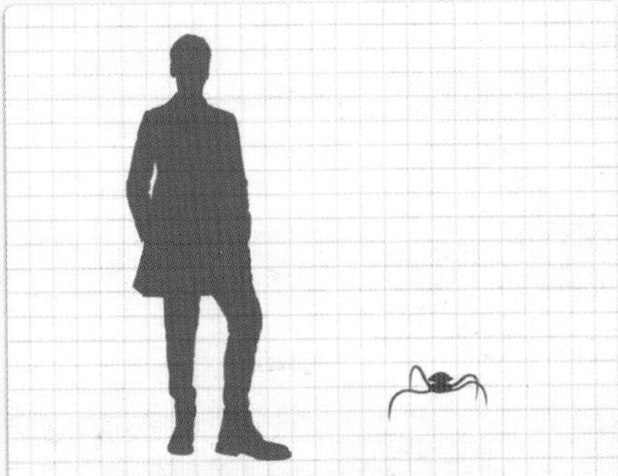

SPEED

SLOW — FAST

0 1 2 3 4 5 6 [7] 8 9 10

DANGEROUS RATING

SAFE — DEADLY

0 1 2 3 4 5 [6] 7 8 9 10

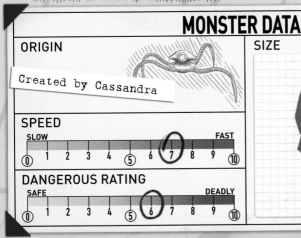

VISITORS TO PLATFORM ONE

I MET ALL SORTS OF ALIENS AND CREATURES ON PLATFORM ONE AT THE END OF THE WORLD. Most of them were perfectly charming. But watch out for the Adherents of the Repeated Meme - they're not at all what they seem . . .

Robes and hoods hide what's underneath.

Bit of bling round the neck. No reason for it, really.

They're robots.

SURVIVAL TIPS

The Adherents of the Repeated Meme were robots. They gave metal spheres as gifts, which hid the robot spiders Cassandra used to sabotage Platform One. So don't accept any presents from them.

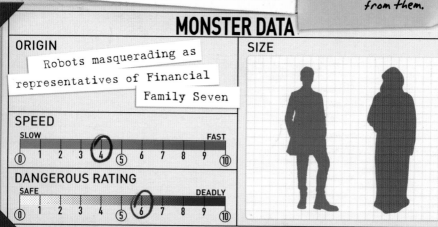

MONSTER DATA

ORIGIN

Robots masquerading as representatives of Financial Family Seven

SIZE

SPEED

SLOW 1 2 3 4 5 6 7 8 9 10 FAST

DANGEROUS RATING

SAFE 1 2 3 4 5 6 7 8 9 10 DEADLY

GRASKE

NAUGHTY LITTLE CREATURES, THE GRASKE. Usually they work for someone else. But they're not above a bit of mischief on their own account. They like to kidnap people - usually children - and replace them with Changelings that they control.

Small, but still dangerous.

Not to be confused with the much nicer Groske.

SURVIVAL TIPS

You might run into Graske drinking in the bar Zaggit Zagoo, or running riot in the Albert Hall during a concert - that's actually my fault. Sorry about that. Don't let one catch you with a cable snare, or who knows where you'll end up.

Ability to disguise itself as a small child.

MONSTER DATA

ORIGIN

Griffoth

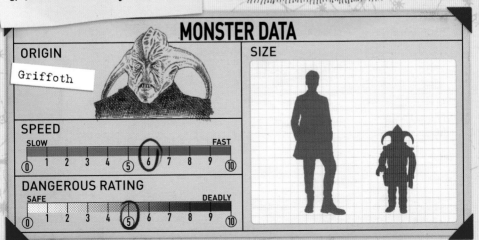

SPEED

SLOW — FAST
0 1 2 3 4 5 6 7 8 9 10

DANGEROUS RATING

SAFE — DEADLY
0 1 2 3 4 5 6 7 8 9 10

SIZE

THE MASTER

NOT ALL MONSTERS LOOK MONSTROUS.
The Master is one of the most monstrous
around - and he's another Time Lord.
Like me, he got bored and left
Gallifrey. But I wanted to explore, to
see things; he just wants to rule the
universe. He delights in other people's
suffering and takes pride in destroying
people and planets.

Renegade Time Lord.

Doesn't look like a monster. But he is.

Carries a laser screwdriver.

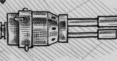

There are other rebellious Time Lords - like the Meddling Monk, or amoral scientist the Rani. But they're nothing like as callous and unpleasant as the Master. Ex-presidents Morbius and Rassilon come close, I suppose. But not that close . . .

SURVIVAL TIPS

A master (pun intended) of disguise, you'll be lucky to spot the Master in a crowd. So best hope he doesn't spot you. Unless you've got a very strong will, he can hypnotise you into doing whatever he wants. Or he might shrink you to death with his Tissue Compression Eliminator.

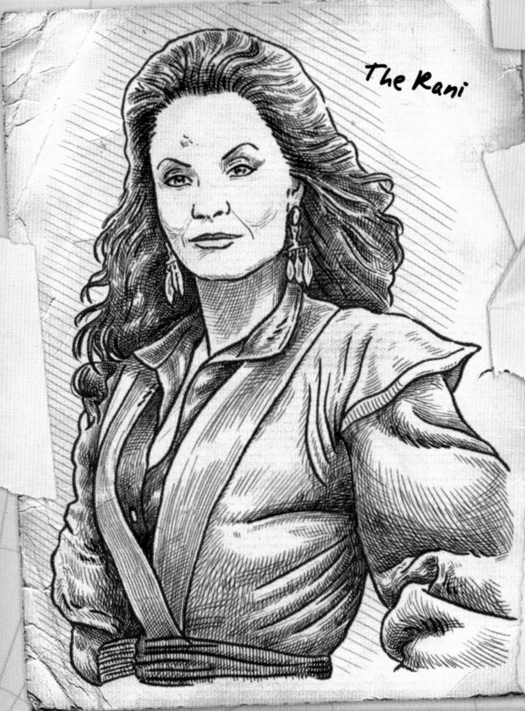
The Rani

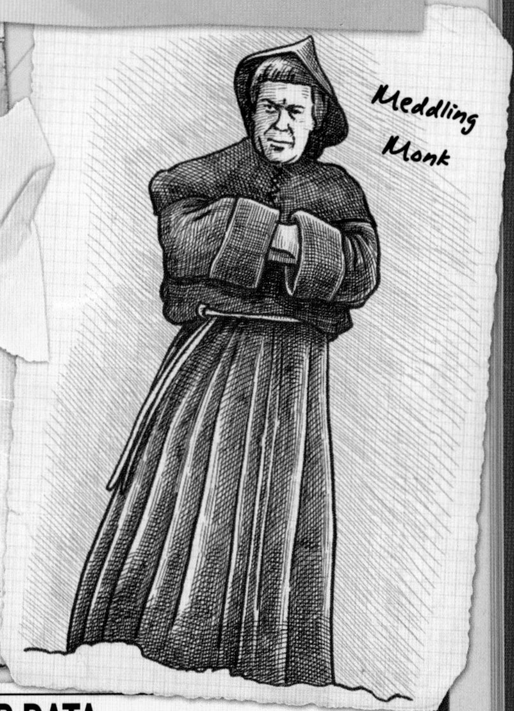
Meddling Monk

MONSTER DATA

ORIGIN

Gallifrey

SPEED

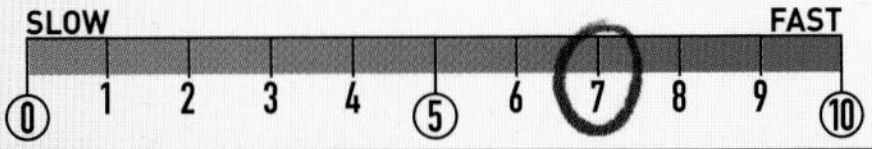
SLOW
FAST
0 1 2 3 4 5 6 7 8 9 10

DANGEROUS RATING

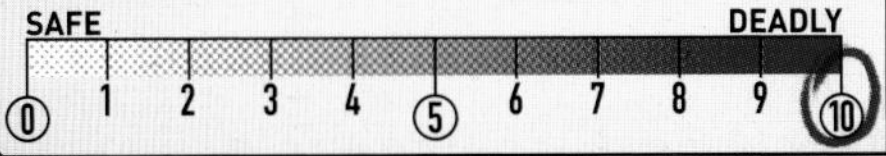
SAFE
DEADLY
0 1 2 3 4 5 6 7 8 9 10

SIZE

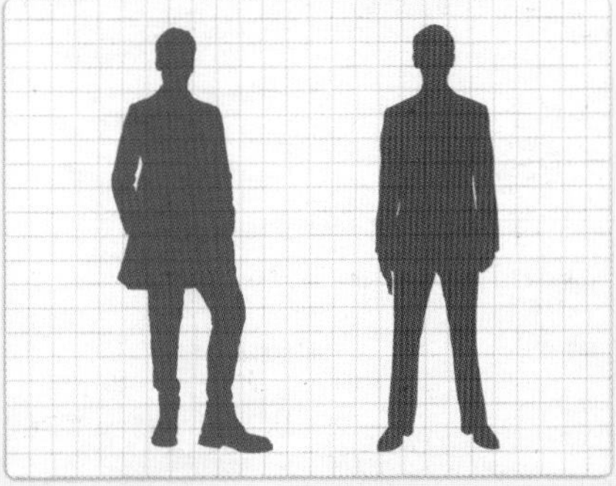

MISSY

MISSY IS SHORT FOR MISTRESS. I should have worked that out, Mistress being the female form of Master. Regenerating into a woman is the ultimate disguise. He's always been a charmer, and Missy is no exception. If she doesn't kill you, she'll probably kiss you. Not sure which is worse.

The Master's a woman. So no beard.

She is completely bananas.

Actually, he didn't always have a beard anyway.

Using stolen Time Lord technology, Missy created the Nethersphere - sometimes misleadingly called 'The Promised Land'. She uploaded the minds of dead people to a Gallifreyan storage system hidden inside St Paul's Cathedral, ready to be downloaded again into Cybermen at her command.

SURVIVAL TIPS

Missy is as dangerous now as when she was the Master, plus she'll get you even when you're dead ... So don't die. That's quite an important one actually. If you do, you'll have to put up with her serving you tea (or worse, kissing you) and then you'll get reincarnated as a Cyberman. Avoid creepy ladies with parasols and a teapot.

MONSTER DATA

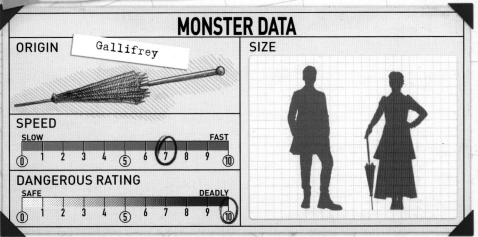

ORIGIN	Gallifrey

SIZE

SPEED

SLOW | | | | | | | | | | FAST
0 1 2 3 4 5 6 7 8 9 10

DANGEROUS RATING

SAFE | | | | | | | | | | DEADLY
0 1 2 3 4 5 6 7 8 9 10

FUTUREKIND

IF FUTUREKIND IS REALLY THE FUTURE OF THE HUMAN RACE, YOU'RE IN BIG TROUBLE. Mutated killer cannibals living like animals on the planet Malcassairo in the far future - not something to look forward to.

More like regression than evolution.

Fanged teeth - do you quite an injury, those could.

Good eyebrows though. They got that right.

SURVIVAL TIPS

Futurekind keep fit by chasing food. So, if you have to run, make sure you're fast, or have somewhere safe to run to. Otherwise you'll be dinner. Safest place on Malcassairo is the human compound - get there quick, and show your teeth.

MONSTER DATA

ORIGIN

Malcassairo

SPEED

SLOW — FAST
⓪ 1 2 3 4 ⑤ 6 ⑦ 8 9 ⑩

DANGEROUS RATING

SAFE — DEADLY
⓪ 1 2 3 4 ⑤ ⑥ 7 8 9 ⑩

SIZE

THE TOCLAFANE

THE VERY LAST HUMANS, AT THE END OF THE UNIVERSE, EVOLVED BEYOND FUTUREKIND INTO THE TOCLAFANE. They're just heads that behave like spoiled children. Inside flying robot spheres armed with knives and lasers. Not a good combination.

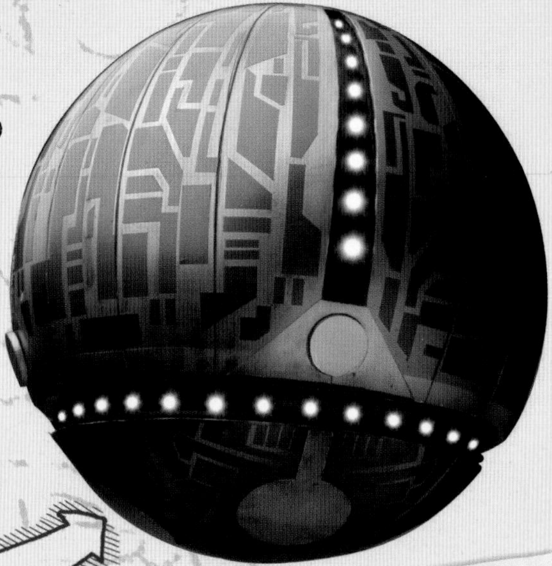

The end of the human race?

They can't half zip about.

Each Toclafane sphere is armed with knives, lasers and other lethal weapons.

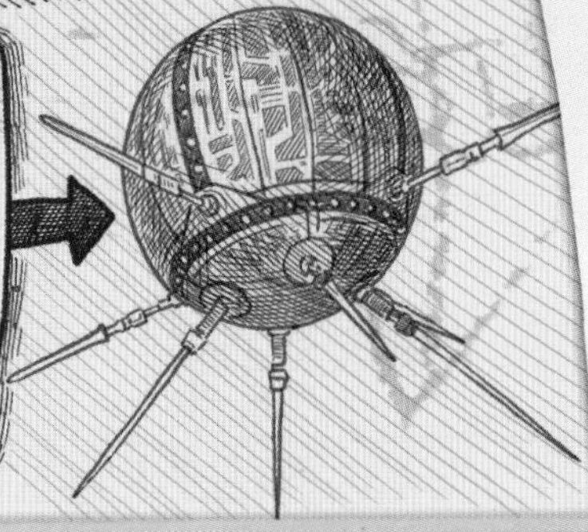

SURVIVAL TIPS

You wouldn't normally have to worry about something so far off in the future. But the Master brought the Toclafane back through time to conquer Earth. A bit hard on their ancestors, I'd have thought.

MONSTER DATA

ORIGIN Utopia, at the end of the Universe, in about 100,000,000,000,000 AD

SIZE

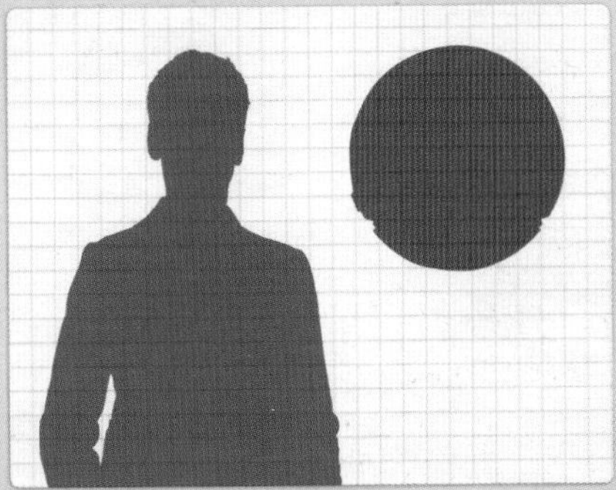

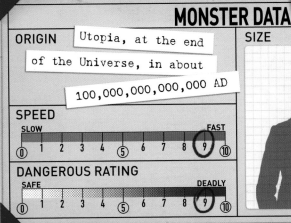

SPEED

SLOW 0 1 2 3 4 5 6 7 8 9 10 FAST — rating circled: 9

DANGEROUS RATING

SAFE 0 1 2 3 4 5 6 7 8 9 10 DEADLY — rating circled: 9

THE GELTH

GASSY CREATURES THAT LOST THEIR PLANET DURING THE TIME WAR. The Gelth use people with psychic abilities to cross the plane into our world. Once here, they possess the dead, bringing them back to zombie-life. The more dead people they find, the better - and you can guess how they do that.

The Gelth are actually hazy, gassy creatures.

SURVIVAL TIPS

Gelth-controlled zombies aren't that fast. But gaseous Gelth can whizz about like - well, like gas. And, being a gas, you can ignite them and blow them up. Stand well clear.

They inhabit the bodies of the dead.

Which can be a bit of a shock when they start walking around.

MONSTER DATA

ORIGIN

Unknown

SPEED

SLOW — FAST
0 1 2 3 4 5 6 7 (8) 9 10

DANGEROUS RATING

SAFE — DEADLY
0 1 2 3 4 5 6 7 (8) 9 10

SIZE

THE JAGAROTH

AN ANCIENT, VICIOUS, WARLIKE RACE WITH GREEN SPAGHETTI HEADS AND ONE EYE. Luckily, they all blew up in a spaceship above prehistoric Earth. Unluckily, the pilot, Scaroth, got splintered through time and tried to go back and stop the explosion.

Scaroth was the last of the Jagaroth.

He got splintered through time, so popped up all over history.

Cunning disguise.

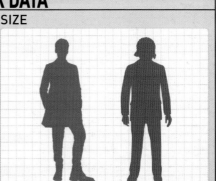

SURVIVAL TIPS

Scaroth turns up throughout history — if you meet a green spaghetti-headed one-eyed gentleman, it's probably him. He'll sacrifice anything to save his race — including you. So be on your guard.

MONSTER DATA

ORIGIN

No idea. Well, it was all a very long time ago

SPEED

SLOW — FAST
0 1 2 3 4 5 6 7 8 9 10

DANGEROUS RATING

SAFE — DEADLY
0 1 2 3 4 5 6 7 8 9 10

SIZE

THE DREAM LORD

THE DREAM LORD PUT ME, AMY AND RORY INSIDE DREAMS WHERE WE COULD END UP DEAD. He was actually psychic pollen feeding on the dark sides of our minds. The Dream Lord himself was from the dark side of my mind. Bit embarrassing . . .

He looks ordinary enough.

Especially considering he doesn't really exist.

Just an upstart speck of pollen.

SURVIVAL TIPS

If you find yourself flitting between different realities, then one may be a psychic-pollen dream world. The tricky thing is working out which is which, so you can wake up and do the dusting.

MONSTER DATA

ORIGIN

The candle meadows of Karass don Slava

SPEED

SLOW 0 1 2 3 4 5 6 7 8 9 10 FAST

DANGEROUS RATING

SAFE 0 1 2 3 4 5 6 7 8 9 10 DEADLY

SIZE

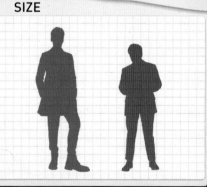

EKNODINES

THE EKNODINES ARE A PROUD AND ANCIENT RACE OF CREATURES THAT INHABIT AND CONTROL OTHER PEOPLE'S BODIES. Watch out for a green eye on a stalk inside a person's mouth. That's not normal - it means they're possessed. Or they could have been a dream.

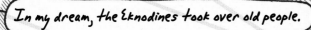

In my dream, the Eknodines took over old people.

They made them healthier.

But it's still possession.

SURVIVAL TIPS

The eye in the mouth is a dead giveaway. Plus all the other usual 'they've been taken over by aliens' clues. Best thing you can do is to wake up. **WAKE UP! NOW!!!**

Fortunately the oldies were quite slow.

MONSTER DATA

ORIGIN

Unknown

SIZE

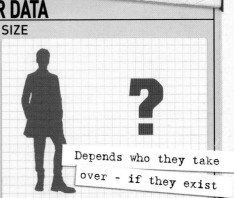

?

Depends who they take over - if they exist

SPEED

SLOW
0 1 2 5 10

Depends who they take over - if they exist

DANGEROUS RATING

SAFE   DEADLY
6 7 8 9 10

If they exist

AXONS

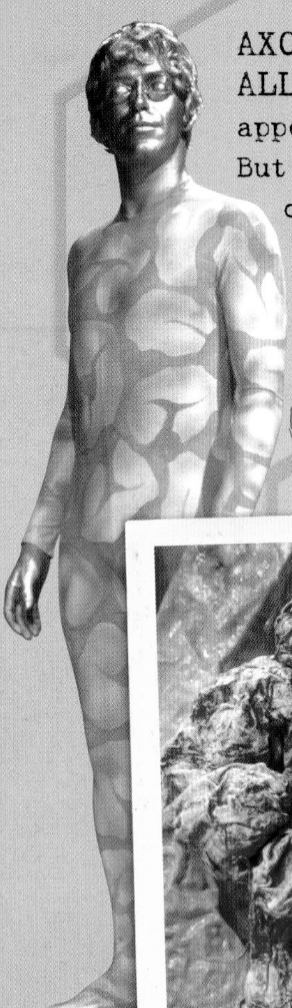

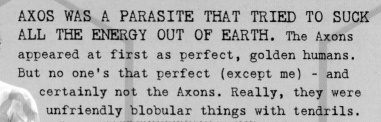

AXOS WAS A PARASITE THAT TRIED TO SUCK ALL THE ENERGY OUT OF EARTH. The Axons appeared at first as perfect, golden humans. But no one's that perfect (except me) - and certainly not the Axons. Really, they were unfriendly blobular things with tendrils.

The Axons pretended to look nice.

But they actually looked like this – the opposite of nice.

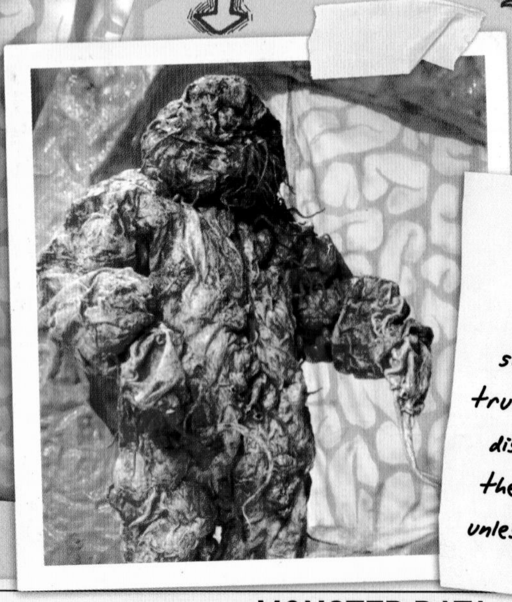

Tendrils pack a powerful punch, and deliver a big electric shock.

SURVIVAL TIPS

The Axons offered Axonite, a miracle substance. But, if something seems too good to be true, it probably is. And, if someone dissolves into a blobby monster, then it's time you were leaving – unless you have a time loop available.

MONSTER DATA

ORIGIN

Axos was all one creature - spaceship and occupants

SPEED

SLOW — FAST

0 1 2 3 4 5 6 7 8 9 10 (7 circled)

DANGEROUS RATING

SAFE — DEADLY

0 1 2 3 4 5 6 7 8 9 10 (7 circled)

SIZE

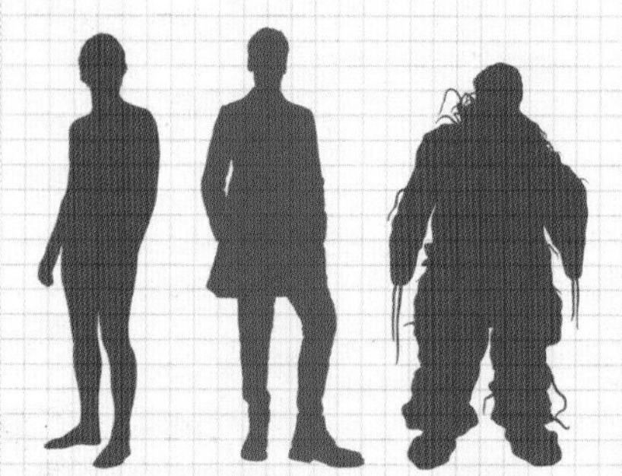

HANDBOTS

ROBOTS WITH BLANK FACES THAT SEE USING THEIR HANDS. Pretty daft. Not actually bad - a robot is only as good or bad as its programming. But they thought Amy had a disease - which she didn't - and their 'cure' would have killed her.

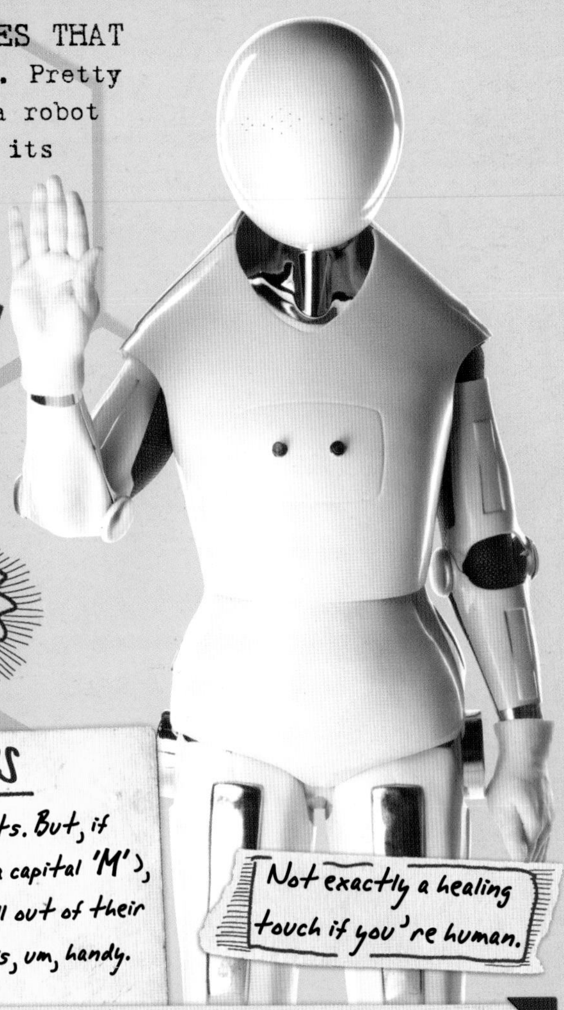

The hands are the most realistic thing about them.

Their hands deliver medicine that can knock you out.

SURVIVAL TIPS

Usually you'll be fine with Handbots. But, if there's a Misunderstanding (with a capital 'M'), don't let them touch you. Keep well out of their way. Or hit them with whatever is, um, handy.

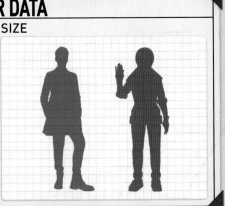

Not exactly a healing touch if you're human.

MONSTER DATA

ORIGIN Two Streams Facility on Apalapucia

SIZE

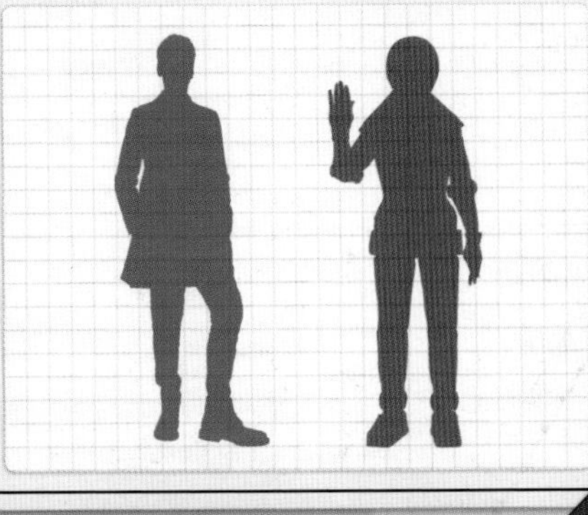

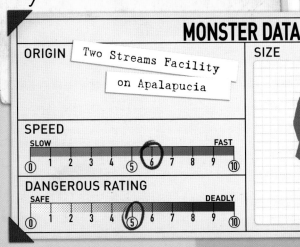

SPEED

SLOW — FAST

0 1 2 3 4 5 (6) 7 8 9 10

DANGEROUS RATING

SAFE — DEADLY

0 1 2 3 4 (5) 6 7 8 9 10

SLITHEEN

A FAMILY DEDICATED TO MAKING MONEY - AND RUTHLESS ABOUT IT. The Slitheen all have long, tricky hyphenated names. They were banished from their own planet - probably because of their business practices, not their long names. They are a nasty, bloodthirsty lot and like hunting humans.

Green, greedy and vicious.

Likes to hunt humans - and anything else, come to that.

Ability to disguise itself as a human.

The Slitheen once tried to persuade you lot that Earth was being invaded. They did this by crashing a spaceship into the clock tower of the Houses of Parliament - a spaceship apparently piloted by a pig. In a spacesuit. And no one spotted it was a hoax. Humans are unbelievable sometimes.

SURVIVAL TIPS

Slitheen can squeeze themselves into human-skin suits. But they have to be big people, as the Slitheen are big, and there are unpleasant farting noises as gas builds up. The gas is caused by calcium decay, and smells like bad breath. If there's a Slitheen after you, chuck vinegar at it. That'll dissolve the calcium and make it explode.

MONSTER DATA

ORIGIN
Raxacoricofallapatorius

SIZE

SPEED
SLOW — FAST
0 1 2 3 4 5 6 7 8 9 10

DANGEROUS RATING
SAFE — DEADLY
0 1 2 3 4 5 6 7 8 9 10

GAS-MASK ZOMBIES

IN WORLD WAR II, AN ALIEN SHIP CRASHED IN LONDON. It was full of nanogenes - tiny particles that 'repaired' wounded people. Except the first person they tried to fix was a boy in a gas mask. They assumed that's what humans were supposed to be like - so everyone they 'mended' became a creature with a gas mask fixed to its face, looking for its mummy.

Gas mask fused to face.

'Repaired' to match the dead boy.

All they say is 'Are you my mummy?'

If they touch you, the nanogenes will probably convert you, too.

The Empty Child, as the street kids called him, was actually Jamie, a boy killed in an air raid. All he really wanted was his mum. I helped him find her, then the nanogenes worked out what humans should really be like and fixed everyone. Job done.

SURVIVAL TIPS

You're probably not up to reprogramming nanogenes. So don't try. Keep away from people in gas masks, unless there's a reason for them to be wearing gas masks. And, if a small child is looking for their mummy, it's a wise idea to help find her. That's just good advice, anyway — even if they're not an alien-mutated resurrected corpse.

MONSTER DATA

ORIGIN

London, 1941

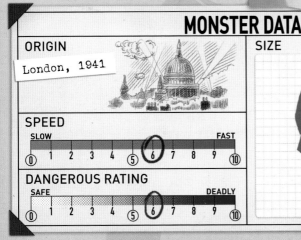

SPEED

SLOW   FAST

0   1   2   3   4   5   6   7   8   9   10

DANGEROUS RATING

SAFE   DEADLY

0   1   2   3   4   5   6   7   8   9   10

SIZE

THE SYCORAX

Helmet made from bone.

Ability to perform blood control.

AN ANCIENT RACE OF BLOODTHIRSTY WARRIORS, THE SYCORAX TRAVEL IN SPACESHIPS MADE OF ROCK. They prefer to conquer by deception, fooling world leaders into surrendering, then enslaving everyone. That horrible face is actually a mask - the really horrible face is underneath.

Trophies from previous battles, like dead enemies' teeth. How pleasant.

SURVIVAL TIPS

If a spaceship that looks like a lump of rock arrives, it's probably the Sycorax. Don't believe their threats. A bit of a sword fight and a blow from a well-aimed tangerine will probably see them off.

MONSTER DATA

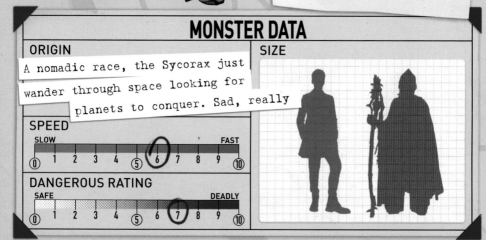

ORIGIN

A nomadic race, the Sycorax just wander through space looking for planets to conquer. Sad, really

SIZE

SPEED

SLOW · · · · · · · · · FAST
⓪ 1 2 3 4 ⑤ ⑥ 7 8 9 ⑩

DANGEROUS RATING

SAFE · · · · · · · · · DEADLY
⓪ 1 2 3 4 ⑤ 6 ⑦ 8 9 ⑩

ROBOFORMS

ROBOT SCAVENGERS. A bit rubbish, to be honest. They have a thing about disguises - perhaps so they don't look like rubbish robots. Killer Christmas tree? Could be a Roboform. Killer Santa Claus? Roboform. I guess they have a thing about Christmas, too. Bizarre.

Not really Santa.

Mask conceals robotic face.

SURVIVAL TIPS

You'd better watch out if a killer-robot Santa Claus is coming to town. And on no account try to give him your Christmas list. Get him to chase you round till his batteries run down.

Musical instruments can shoot fire.

MONSTER DATA

ORIGIN

Scavengers with no fixed abode

SIZE

SPEED

SLOW · 0 1 2 3 4 5 6 7 8 9 10 · FAST

DANGEROUS RATING

SAFE · 0 1 2 3 4 5 6 7 8 9 10 · DEADLY

THE JAGRAFESS

ITS FULL NAME IS THE MIGHTY JAGRAFESS OF THE HOLY HADROJASSIC MAXARODENFOE. With a name like that, you can tell it's big - with an even bigger mouth. It hung from the ceiling of the top floor of Satellite Five, and tried to shape humanity's development by deciding what news to broadcast.

Huge - it covers the ceiling.

It probably is the ceiling.

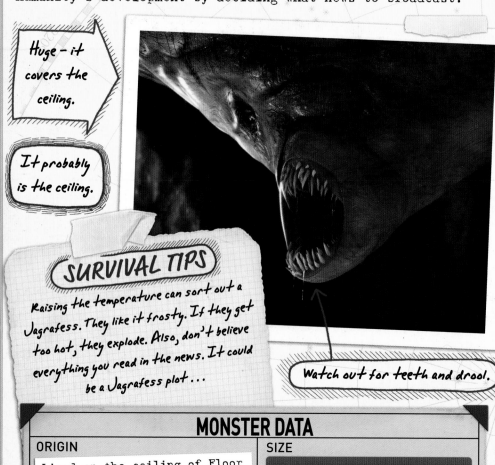

SURVIVAL TIPS

Raising the temperature can sort out a Jagrafess. They like it frosty. If they get too hot, they explode. Also, don't believe everything you read in the news. It could be a Jagrafess plot...

Watch out for teeth and drool.

MONSTER DATA

ORIGIN

Lived on the ceiling of Floor 500 of Satellite Five

SPEED

SLOW — FAST
(0) (1) 2 3 4 (5) 6 7 8 9 (10)

DANGEROUS RATING

SAFE — DEADLY
(0) 1 2 3 4 (5) 6 (7) 8 9 (10)

SIZE

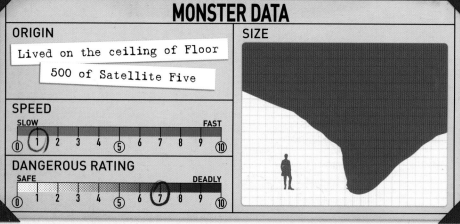

THE WIRE

IF THE WIRE IS IN YOUR TELLY, IT COULD SUCK YOUR FACE OFF AND LEAVE YOU WITH NO WILL. It came to Earth when its own kind denied it a body. Now it's after the life essence of everyone who watches television.

It might look like a nice old-fashioned TV announcer . . .

But it's not.

The Wire 'infected' TVs sold by Mr Magpie in 1953.

SURVIVAL TIPS

Is that TV announcer or newsreader behaving a bit oddly? Talking directly to YOU? If you got your TV from Magpie Electricals, that might be the Wire – after your life essence. Time to change channel or you'll lose your face.

MONSTER DATA

ORIGIN

Hermethica

SIZE

SPEED

SLOW — FAST

0 1 2 3 4 5 6 7 8 9 10 (10 circled)

DANGEROUS RATING

SAFE — DEADLY

0 1 2 3 4 5 6 7 8 9 10 (8 circled)

HOIX

VERY AGGRESSIVE ALIENS. Definitely pudding-brains.
Rose and I ran into a Hoix in London once. Managed to tempt
it with a pork chop before it could cause too much trouble.
Saw it off. Job done.

Alien.

Angry.

Likes to eat
raw meat.

YOU ARE RAW MEAT.

SURVIVAL TIPS

Hot liquid usually deals with a
Hoix. You have to get the right
sort of hot liquid, though.
Red-hot liquid will work. Blue,
not so much – in fact, not
at all. Don't use blue.

MONSTER DATA

ORIGIN: Unknown

SIZE

SPEED

SLOW — FAST
0 1 2 3 4 5 6 7 (8) 9 10

DANGEROUS RATING

SAFE — DEADLY
0 1 2 3 4 5 (6) 7 8 9 10

THE KRYNOID

THE KRYNOID IS A PLANT - BUT IT'S NOT LIKE THE SORT OF PLANTS YOU HAVE IN YOUR GARDEN. I'm assuming you have a garden. Usually, animals eat plants. But, on planets where the Krynoid grows, the plants eat the animals.

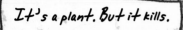

It's a plant. But it kills.

And it can channel its power into other plants . . .

So that they kill too.

SURVIVAL TIPS

When your plants start to come alive – like, moving about trying to kill you alive, not just sprouting flowers and stuff – there's a Krynoid about. Weed killer is your best bet here.

MONSTER DATA

ORIGIN Come from a volcanic world - the eruptions shoot Krynoid pods off into space

SIZE They start smaller - just as pods - but they end up big.

SPEED

SLOW 0 1 2 (3) 4 5 6 7 8 9 10 FAST — circled: 3

DANGEROUS RATING

SAFE 0 1 2 3 4 5 6 7 (8) 9 10 DEADLY — circled: 8

THE ZYGONS

ORANGE SHAPE-SHIFTERS COVERED IN SUCKERS. Their planet was destroyed when a star blew up, so now they think Earth would be a good homeworld. They'd like to change the climate and bring in huge Skarasen creatures like savage dinosaurs. They kept one in Loch Ness, which explains a lot.

It can disguise itself as a human. Or a horse. Or any animal, really.

Zygon warlords have bigger suckers on their heads.

Zygons can sting with their hands. Painful.

A group of stranded Zygons kept their Skarasen in Loch Ness. It's an armoured cyborg - part robot, part living creature. The Zygons needed it for milk to survive, but they also used it to destroy oil rigs in the North Sea and generally cause trouble.

SURVIVAL TIPS

If there's a rampaging dinosaur-like creature on the loose, there may be Zygons about, too. So, if your best friend is behaving oddly or starts to blur in front of your eyes, it might be best to give them a bit of alone time, know what I mean? And call in UNIT.

MONSTER DATA

ORIGIN | Since their planet blew up, they live in a vast fleet of refugee spaceships

SPEED

SLOW — 0 1 2 3 4 (5) 6 7 8 9 10 — FAST

DANGEROUS RATING

SAFE — 0 1 2 3 4 (5) 6 7 8 (9) 10 — DEADLY

SIZE

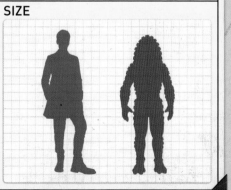

ELEMENTAL SHADE

A LIVING SHADOW. And not a nice one. I was attacked by an Elemental Shade that had escaped from the Howling Halls. I finally stopped it, but not before it killed a woman.

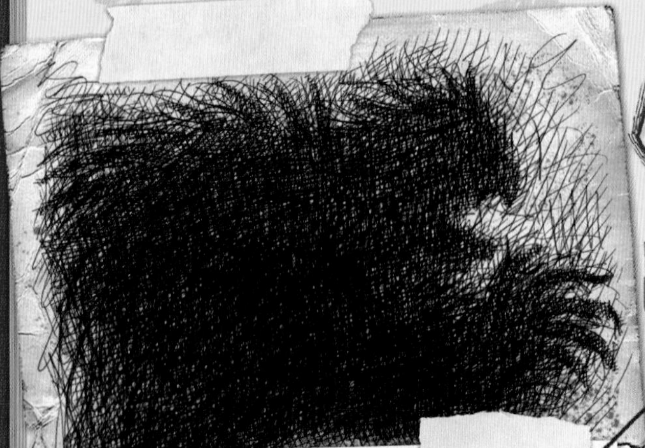

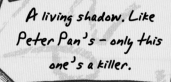

A living shadow. Like Peter Pan's – only this one's a killer.

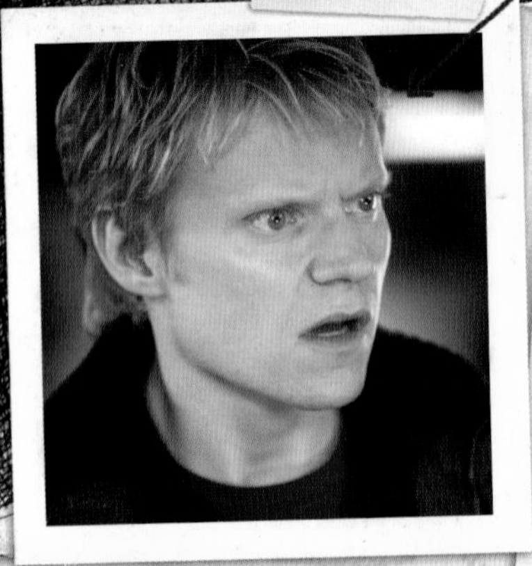

Elton Pope saw me in his house the night the Elemental Shade killed his mum.

SURVIVAL TIPS

How do you get rid of a shadow? Any shadow, living or just shadowy? Light is the answer. So, if the shadows come after you, shine a light at them. The brighter the better.

MONSTER DATA

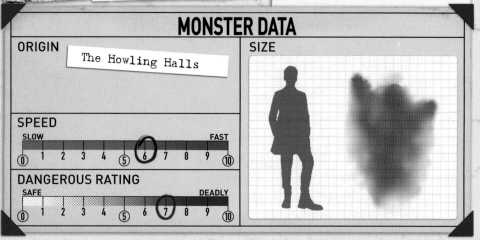

ORIGIN

The Howling Halls

SPEED

SLOW — FAST

0 1 2 3 4 5 6 7 8 9 10 (6 circled)

DANGEROUS RATING

SAFE — DEADLY

0 1 2 3 4 5 6 7 8 9 10 (7 circled)

SIZE

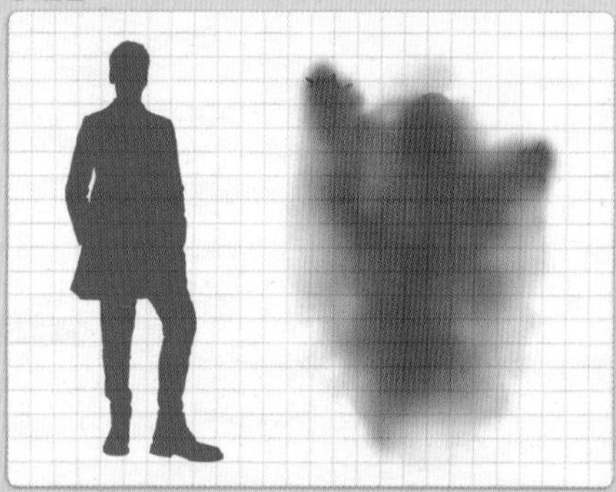

ABZORBALOFF

THE ABZORBALOFF EATS PEOPLE. But not in the way you think - it absorbs them (as in Abzorb-aloff, OK?). See an Abzorbaloff in its true form, and faces and bits of the people it's absorbed will be sticking out of its skin. Rather horrid, really.

The Abzorbaloff can disguise itself as a human.

Faces of its victims remain visible in its skin for a while.

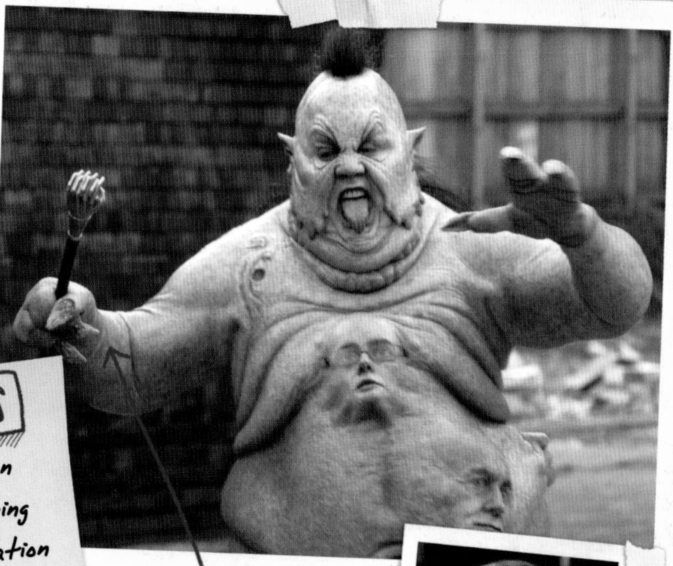

SURVIVAL TIPS

Not much you can do once an Abzorbaloff starts absorbing you. But, destroy his Limitation Field, and the absorbed people trying to get out again will make him explode. Stand well back - it could get gooey.

Its cane is actually a Limitation-Field Creator.

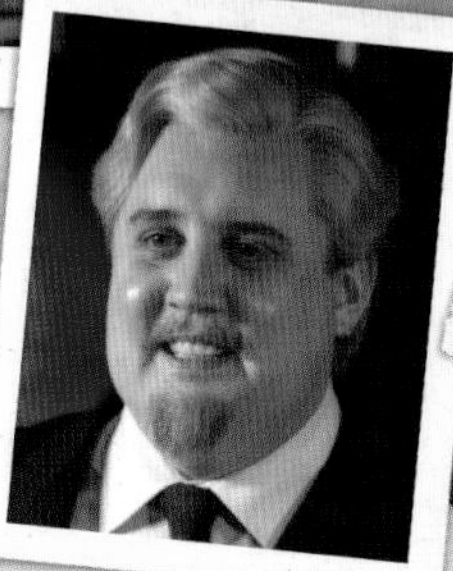

MONSTER DATA

ORIGIN

Clom - twin world to Raxacoricofallapatorius

SIZE

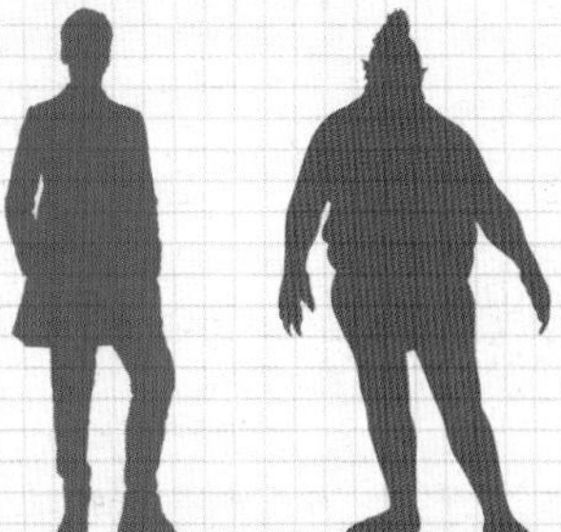

SPEED

SLOW 0 1 2 3 4 (5) 6 7 8 9 10 FAST

DANGEROUS RATING

SAFE 0 1 2 3 4 5 (6) 7 8 9 10 DEADLY

VASHTA NERADA

ALSO KNOWN AS THE
PIRANHAS OF THE AIR, OR
THE SHADOWS THAT EAT THE
FLESH. They hide in darkness
- in fact, they are darkness.
And they can eat the flesh
off a person in a second,
leaving just bones behind.

SURVIVAL TIPS

If you have an extra shadow, that could be the Vashta Nerada. If it is, then it's too late. But, if you see someone else with too many shadows, get into the light. Now!

Can munch the flesh off any living thing in a few seconds.

Avoid stepping into the shadows.

MONSTER DATA

ORIGIN

Forests and woods

SPEED

SLOW ——————————————— FAST
0 1 2 3 4 5 6 7 8 9 10

DANGEROUS RATING

SAFE ——————————————— DEADLY
0 1 2 3 4 5 6 7 8 9 10

SIZE

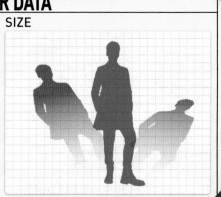

SPACESUIT ZOMBIES

IN THE FUTURE THERE ARE THOUGHT-MAILS. And, if the Vashta Nerada munch your body while you're sending a thought-mail, your last thoughts will linger after you're dead, as a Data Ghost. You'll linger, too, sort of - as a zombie skeleton.

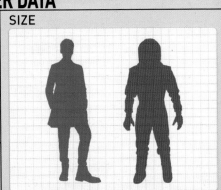

Spacesuit untouched by the Vashta Nerada.

Skeleton is all that's left of the original occupant.

SURVIVAL TIPS

If a spacesuit comes at you, check the helmet. Look inside. Friend of yours? Probably all right then. Skull? Probably not. But you should have time to hide. Probably.

Lots of shadows, probably. Only one is real.

MONSTER DATA

ORIGIN

The Library

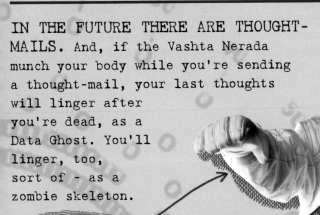

SPEED

SLOW — 0 1 2 3 **4** (5) 6 7 8 9 10 — FAST

DANGEROUS RATING

SAFE — 0 1 2 3 4 (5) 6 7 **8** 9 10 — DEADLY

SIZE

THE SUN-POSSESSED

DON'T MESS WITH THE SUN-POSSESSED. The crew of the SS Pentallian used a fusion scoop to steal some of the energy from a sun. Not wise. The living sun turned a couple of the crew into Sun-Possessed zombies - one touch, and WOOMF! Burned up.

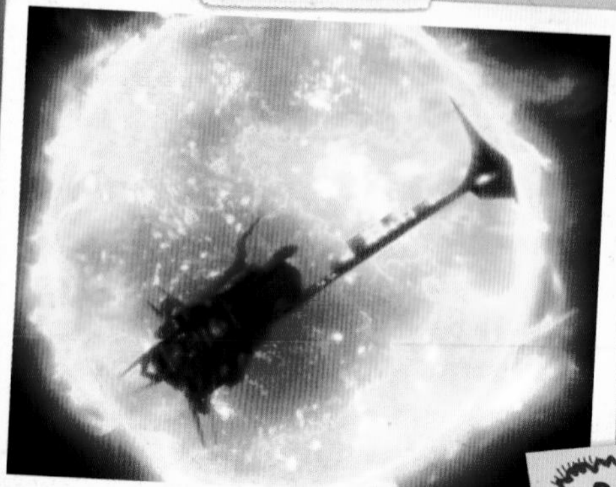

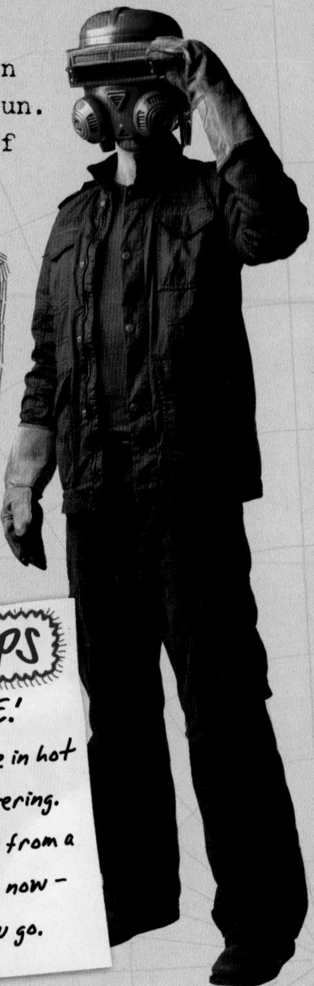

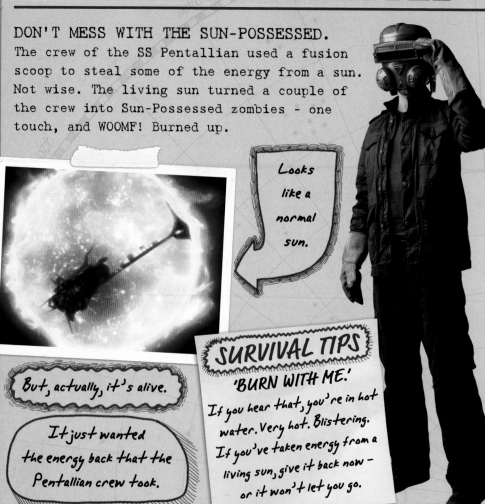

Looks like a normal sun.

But, actually, it's alive.

It just wanted the energy back that the Pentallian crew took.

SURVIVAL TIPS

'BURN WITH ME.'

If you hear that, you're in hot water. Very hot. Blistering. If you've taken energy from a living sun, give it back now – or it won't let you go.

MONSTER DATA

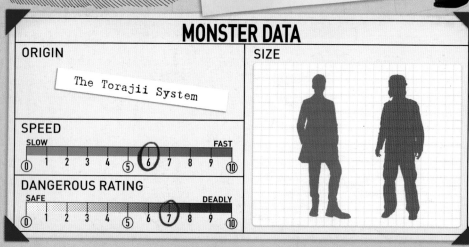

ORIGIN

The Torajii System

SPEED

SLOW 0 1 2 3 4 5 [6] 7 8 9 10 FAST

DANGEROUS RATING

SAFE 0 1 2 3 4 5 6 [7] 8 9 10 DEADLY

SIZE

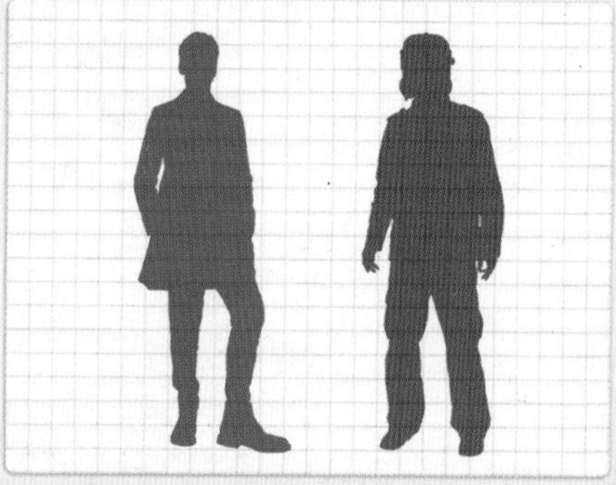

TIME ZOMBIES

THE EYE OF HARMONY IS WHAT POWERS THE TARDIS. It's not to be messed with, or you could end up with burned skin and your insides turned to liquid. Not a good thing. Especially as you're still alive - sort of.

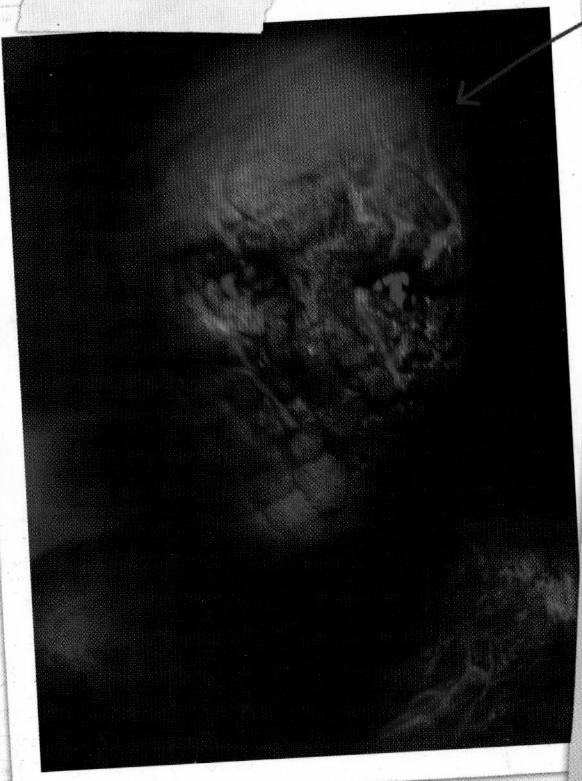

Burned skin.

Mushy insides.

Don't mess with TARDIS stuff you don't understand.

SURVIVAL TIPS

Clara and I once met Time Zombie versions of ourselves. Since it was actually before we became Time Zombies, we changed things so we never got zombie-fied. But, simple rule: Don't. Mess. With. The. TARDIS. Got it? Good.

MONSTER DATA

ORIGIN

Exposure to the Eye of Harmony

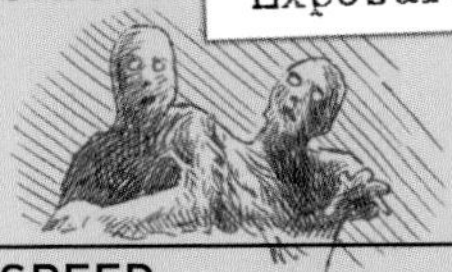

SIZE

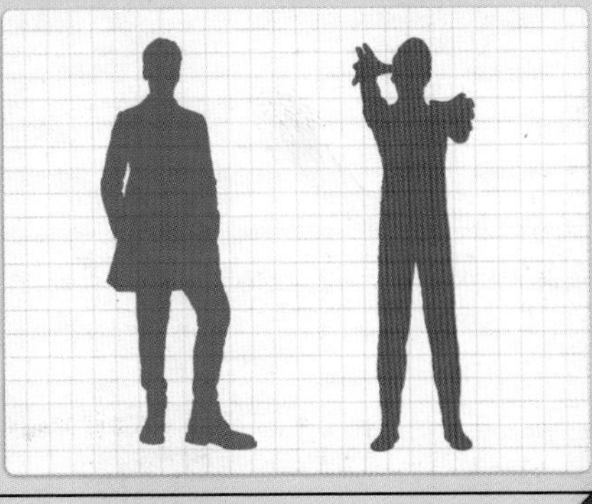

SPEED

SLOW — FAST

0 1 2 3 4 5 6 7 8 9 10 (6 circled)

DANGEROUS RATING

SAFE — DEADLY

0 1 2 3 4 5 6 7 8 9 10 (7 circled)

ISOLUS

THE ISOLUS DRIFT THROUGH SPACE, USING IONIC POWER
TO CREATE MAKE-BELIEVE WORLDS IN WHICH TO PLAY.
This is a problem if an Isolus gets stranded - the things
it might create from other people's thoughts and fears can
be quite unpleasant.

An Isolus child
stranded on Earth
befriended Chloe Webber.

It made her
pictures come to life
– even her scribbles.

Nightmares about her cruel,
dead father came to life too...

SURVIVAL TIPS

A stranded Isolus may pick
up on your fears. Think happy
thoughts. Be nice to people –
even the stupid ones.
If your drawings come alive,
you need to be even nicer.
Good luck with that.

MONSTER DATA

ORIGIN

Unknown

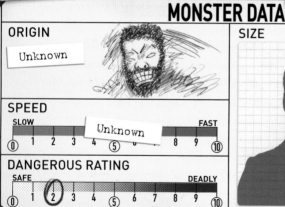

SPEED

SLOW									FAST
⓪	1	2	3	4	⑤		8	9	⑩

Unknown

DANGEROUS RATING

SAFE									DEADLY
⓪	1	②	3	4	⑤	6	7	8	9	⑩

SIZE

MR SWEET

MR SWEET DIDN'T REALLY EXIST. It was a name made up by a Victorian woman called Winifred Gillyflower for a creature from the late-Cretaceous period of prehistory. Like a big red leech, it was attached to the woman's chest. Sharp teeth and spiky little arms.

Horrid little thing.

Wanted to change the world so people died and it lived.

Mr Sweet was a menace to the Silurians too.

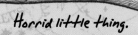

SURVIVAL TIPS

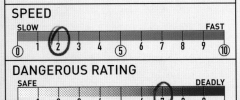

Once you've realised there's a prehistoric leech creature around, you'll also notice it's only small. So rip it away from whoever he's latched on to, and squish him with a stick or stamp on him.

MONSTER DATA

ORIGIN

Earth
- late-Cretaceous period

SIZE

SPEED

SLOW ————————— FAST
⓪ 1 ②️ 3 4 ⑤ 6 7 8 9 ⑩

DANGEROUS RATING

SAFE ————————— DEADLY
⓪ 1 2 3 4 ⑤ 6 ⑦ 8 9 ⑩

123

THE FAMILY OF BLOOD

THEY DIDN'T LIVE LONG - THAT WAS THEIR PROBLEM. So they decided to steal my life energy and live forever - that was my problem. I tried to hide from them, but they found me living as a school teacher on Earth in 1913. By the time they realised I'd hidden to save them not me, it was too late. For them.

Mother of Mine.

Father of Mine.

Son of Mine.

Daughter of Mine.

Looks like a normal family - but they're aliens who've stolen those forms.

And what's with all this 'of Mine' rubbish?

I tried to warn them, but they wouldn't back off. So I bound Father of Mine with unbreakable chains, forged in the heart of a dwarf star. I threw Mother of Mine into a collapsing black hole. I suspended Son of Mine in time as a scarecrow, and I trapped Daughter of Mine inside every mirror. For all eternity. With a balloon.

SURVIVAL TIPS

The Family of Blood shouldn't cause trouble now. Though, if you see a scarecrow moving, that might be a clue one of them has escaped. But, if you catch a glimpse of a little girl with a red balloon looking back at you from the corner of a mirror, don't worry – it means Daughter of Mine is still trapped inside.

MONSTER DATA

ORIGIN: Unknown

SIZE

SPEED

SLOW – FAST

0 1 2 3 4 5 6 7 8 9 10 (6 circled)

DANGEROUS RATING

SAFE – DEADLY

0 1 2 3 4 5 6 7 8 9 10 (8 circled)

SCARECROWS

THE FAMILY OF BLOOD
(turn back a page if
you don't know what I'm
talking about - why don't
you read this book in
the right order?) used
molecular fringe animation
to bring scarecrows to
life. Scary and dangerous.

Clothes made from old sacks.

Cut-out eyes and mouth.

Bodies stuffed with straw.

SURVIVAL TIPS

Anything brought to life by molecular fringe animation will stop being 'alive' when the animator is taken care of. So, look for whoever's animating it. Unless it's plastic - then, look for the Nestene Consciousness.

It's a scarecrow. But brought to life.

MONSTER DATA

ORIGIN

Animated by the Family of Blood

SPEED

SLOW — FAST
0 1 2 3 4 (5) 6 7 8 9 (10)

DANGEROUS RATING

SAFE — DEADLY
0 1 2 3 4 (5) 6 7 8 9 (10)

SIZE

GANTOK

NEVER TRUST A MAN WITH AN EYEPATCH.
Like Gantok. I let him win at chess,
fair and square, in return for taking
me to see Dorium Maldovar. But he
double-crossed me. Actually, I wore
an eyepatch once. You can trust me.

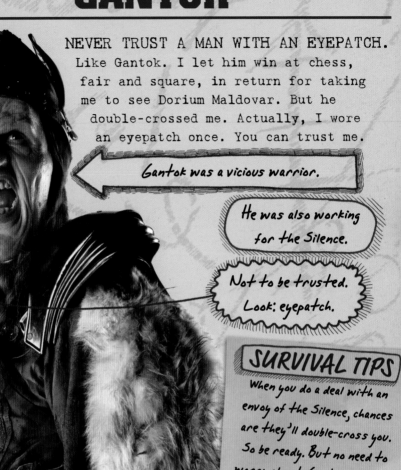

Gantok was a vicious warrior.

He was also working for the Silence.

Not to be trusted.
Look: eyepatch.

SURVIVAL TIPS

When you do a deal with an
envoy of the Silence, chances
are they'll double-cross you.
So be ready. But no need to
worry about Gantok - he was
devoured by the carnivorous
skulls guarding the Seventh
Transept. Good thing, too.

MONSTER DATA

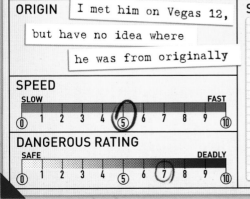

ORIGIN I met him on Vegas 12, but have no idea where he was from originally

SPEED

SLOW   FAST

0   1   2   3   4   (5)   6   7   8   9   10

DANGEROUS RATING

SAFE   DEADLY

0   1   2   3   4   (5)   6   (7)   8   9   10

SIZE

WEEPING ANGELS

ALSO KNOWN AS THE LONELY ASSASSINS, THE WEEPING ANGELS ARE A SNEAKY LOT. They make no noise, just creep about when no one's looking - really, when no one's looking. One touch from an Angel can send you back into the past, so you'll die before you were even born. Then the Angels will feed on the life you might have lived.

Looks like a statue - but it isn't.

They hide their eyes so they don't look at each other.

If anyone is watching, they can't move.

They're pretty quick when no one's looking, though.

DON'T BLINK!

There were four Weeping Angels at a house called Wester Drumlins. It was supposed to be haunted; people went missing. Well, that's not surprising really. They weren't 'missing' - they were touched by an Angel, and sent back in time . . .

MONSTER DATA

ORIGIN
Unknown - they're as old as the universe itself

SIZE

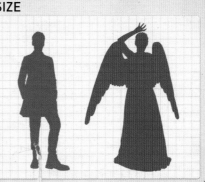

SPEED
SLOW · 0 · 1 · 2 · 3 · 4 · (5) · 6 · 7 · (8) · 9 · (10) · FAST

DANGEROUS RATING
SAFE · (0) · 1 · 2 · 3 · 4 · (5) · 6 · 7 · 8 · (9) · (10) · DEADLY

MAX CAPRICORN

THERE'S NOT A LOT OF MAX CAPRICORN LEFT, EXCEPT HIS HEAD. It's built into a motorised trolley that keeps him alive - if you can call moping about as a trolley-head 'alive'. He tried to crash his spaceship Titanic into Earth.

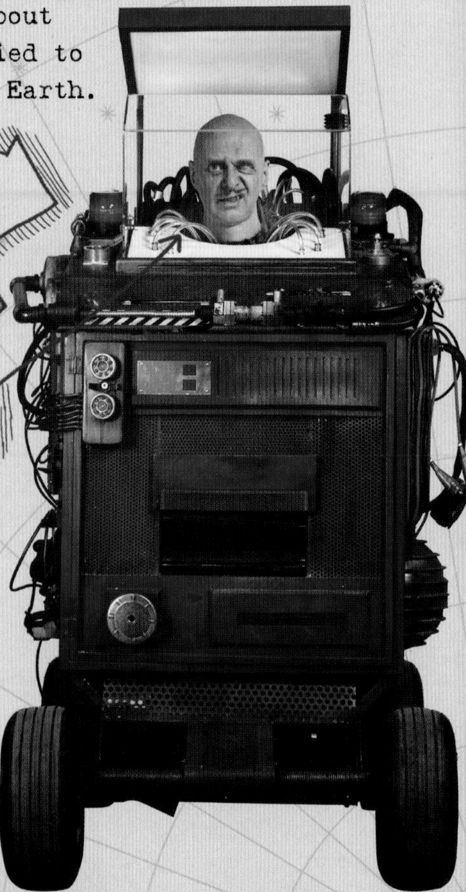

Mobile life support.

It's a glorified trolley, isn't it? I mean, look.

Max's head is all that's left of him.

Wasn't worth keeping, if you ask me.

SURVIVAL TIPS

Max Capricorn hid on the Titanic, plotting against his enemies. He's a plausible salesman, so don't get taken in – he'll kill you if there's a profit in it. Try and push him down a hole.

MONSTER DATA

ORIGIN

Sto

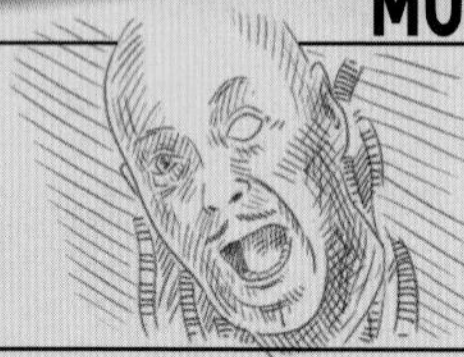

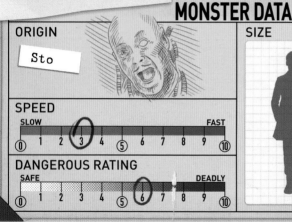

SPEED

SLOW — FAST

0 1 2 [3] 4 5 6 7 8 9 10

DANGEROUS RATING

SAFE — DEADLY

0 1 2 3 4 5 [6] 7 8 9 10

SIZE

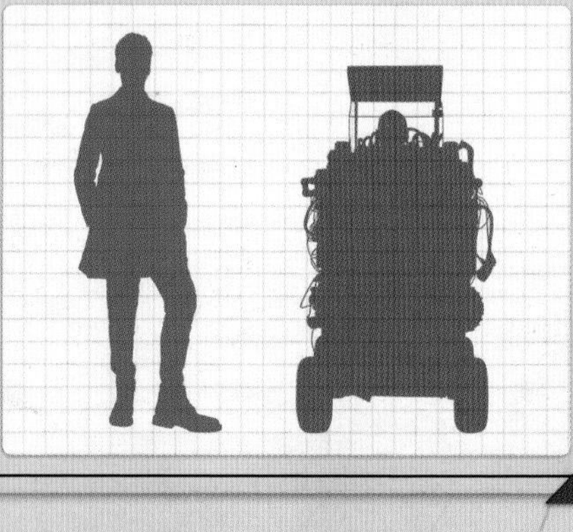

HEAVENLY HOST

THEY LOOK LIKE ANGELS - HENCE THE NAME. Usually they're all right. They're intelligent information systems on board Max Capricorn's spaceliners. But, on the Titanic, Capricorn reprogrammed them to kill the passengers - can't imagine that scored very well on the customer-satisfaction survey.

Look like angels, but actually robots.

Halo can be used as a weapon. Deadly frisbee!

They can fly, too. Really.

SURVIVAL TIPS

If your starliner's robotic information system stops helping and tries to kill you instead, you're in trouble. An electro-magnetic pulse will stop them. Or they obey whoever's the most senior person, so pretend that's you.

MONSTER DATA

ORIGIN

Information systems on board Capricorn spaceliners

SPEED

SLOW | | | | | | | | | FAST
0 1 2 3 4 5 6 7 8 9 10

DANGEROUS RATING

SAFE | | | | | | | | | DEADLY
0 1 2 3 4 5 6 7 8 9 10

SIZE

ADIPOSE

LUMPS OF FAT, WITH LEGS AND LITTLE ARMS AND BEADY LITTLE EYES. And a tooth. The Adipose aren't bad or unpleasant in themselves, but Matron Cofelia used people's body fat to make them - and not just spare fat, either. All of it.

FAT.

With arms, legs, eyes and a tooth.

That's it.

SURVIVAL TIPS

Adipose Industries reduced people's fat by turning it into Adipose. If you're offered a weight-loss product that seems too good to be true, then maybe it is. Try lots of exercise and healthy eating instead. Fruit and veg - only way.

MONSTER DATA

ORIGIN

Adipose 3

SPEED

SLOW | FAST
0 1 2 3 4 5 6 7 8 9 10

DANGEROUS RATING

SAFE | DEADLY
0 1 2 3 4 5 6 7 8 9 10

SIZE

IN HONOUR AND TRADITION. Women aren't allowed to speak at court, but apart from a few weird things like that the Draconians are pretty advanced. For a while, humans and Draconians were at war.

Reptilian skin and appearance.

Shoulders show rank – if they're turned up, that Draconian is important.

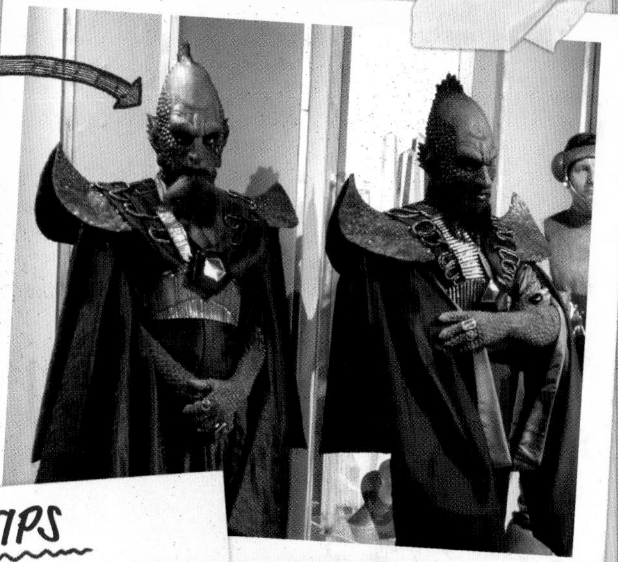

SURVIVAL TIPS

If you meet them when Earth and Draconia were at war, then that could be dicey – or when the Master tricked humans and Draconians into thinking they were attacking each other. But Draconians are generally OK, so try talking to them. Make a new friend.

The traditional Draconian greeting is 'My life at your command'.

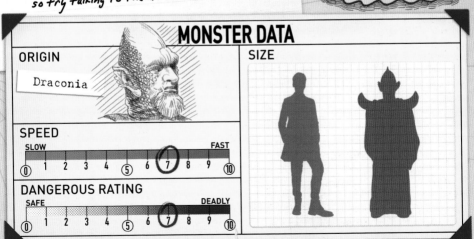

MONSTER DATA

ORIGIN

Draconia

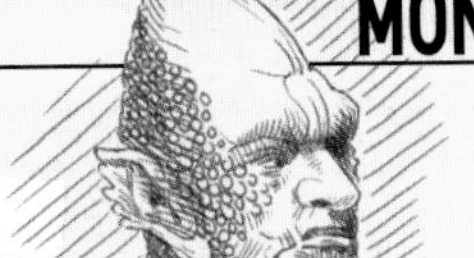

SPEED

SLOW – FAST

0 1 2 3 4 5 6 7 8 9 10 (7 circled)

DANGEROUS RATING

SAFE – DEADLY

0 1 2 3 4 5 6 7 8 9 10 (7 circled)

SIZE

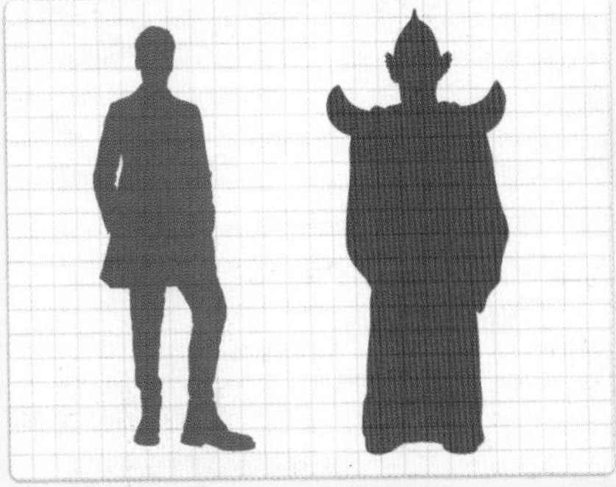

THAT'S THE SONTARANS. They're a clone race - all identical - and they're dedicated to war. That's all they do, all they live (and die) for: war. They've been at war for thousands of years, mainly against the Rutans in a conflict that shows no signs of ending any time soon. Or ever.

Looks rather like a troll.

Only three fingers on each hand.

Rugged space armour.

Short - but don't make fun of its height.

The Rutans, ancient enemies of the Sontarans, are from a cold, icy planet called Ruta-3. They look like squishy green jellyfish with tendrils, and originally evolved in the sea. Be warned - those tendrils pack a punch, as well as an electric current!

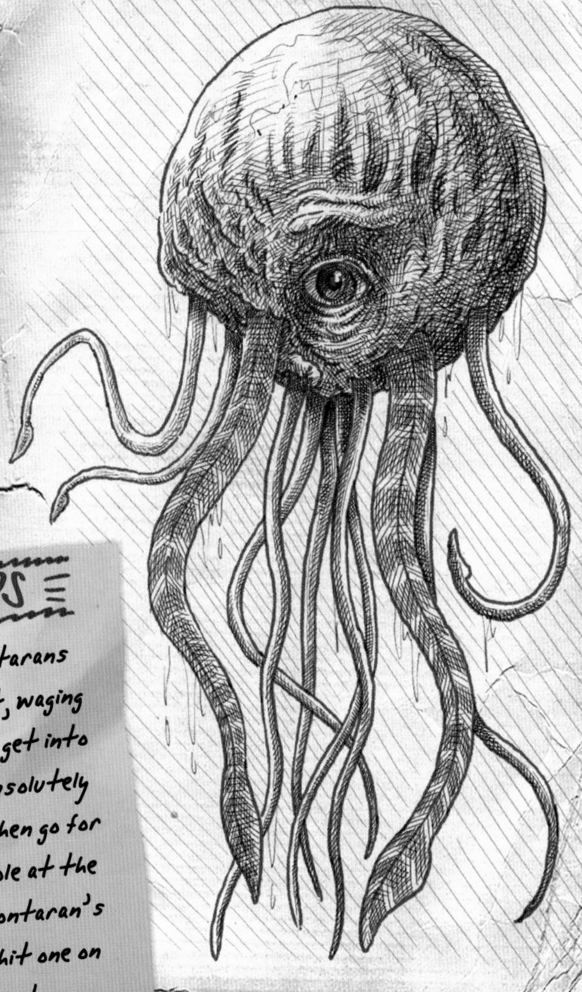

SURVIVAL TIPS

You'll probably know if Sontarans are around – stomping about, waging war and killing people. Don't get into a fight with them unless absolutely necessary. But, if you do, then go for the probic vent – a small hole at the back of the neck. It's a Sontaran's weak point, so, if you can hit one on it, you can knock it out.

MONSTER DATA

ORIGIN

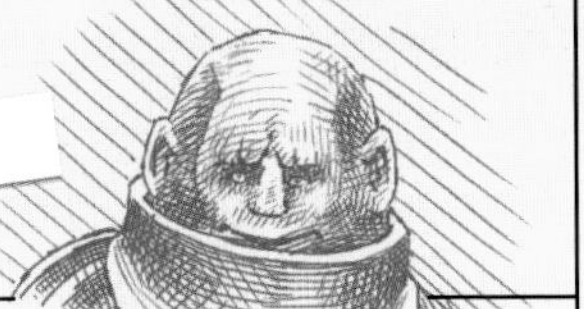

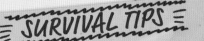

Sontar

SPEED

SLOW — FAST

0 1 2 3 4 5 (6) 7 8 9 10

DANGEROUS RATING

SAFE — DEADLY

0 1 2 3 4 5 6 7 (8) 9 10

SIZE

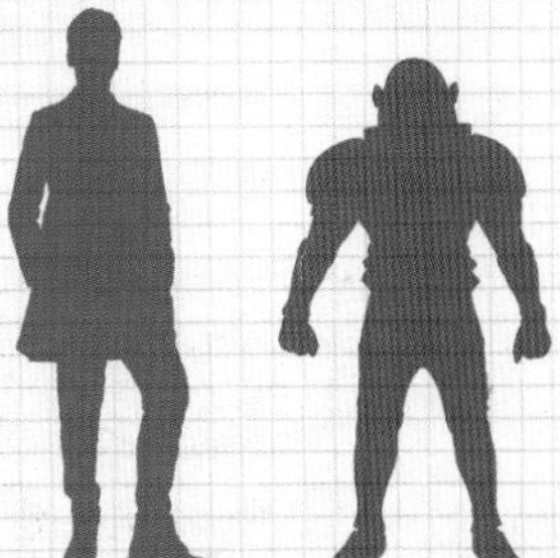

REAPERS

THE REAPERS ARE DRAWN TO PLACES WHERE TIME IS DAMAGED. They cluster like bacteria on a wound, except they sterilise the area - by destroying everything in and around the damage. Not good if you're one of the things that gets sterilised.

Reapers are drawn to anywhere that time has gone wrong.

Anything they 'sterilise' is taken out of time, like it never existed.

Claws can rip through anything - metal, stone, you.

SURVIVAL TIPS

The only way to escape the Reapers is to 'cure' the wound in time. If it's a time paradox - something that shouldn't happen - then it needs sorting out. Fast.

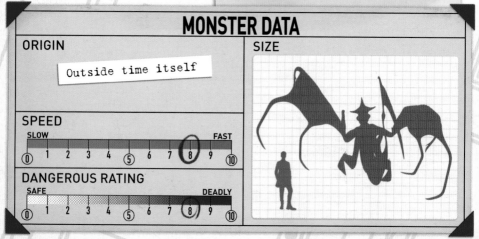

MONSTER DATA

ORIGIN

Outside time itself

SIZE

SPEED

SLOW — FAST
0 1 2 3 4 5 6 7 8 9 10

DANGEROUS RATING

SAFE — DEADLY
0 1 2 3 4 5 6 7 8 9 10

TERILEPTILS

MOST TERILEPTILS ARE ALL RIGHT - IT'S THEIR CRIMINALS YOU HAVE TO WATCH OUT FOR. They look like someone crossed an upright, two-legged reptile with a fish. The Terileptils are noted lovers of beautiful art and things. Probably making up for how they look.

Terileptils' colouring varies.

Scarring can be caused by working in tinclavic mines on Raaga.

They breathe soliton gas.

SURVIVAL TIPS

If you find a soliton-gas generator, chances are the Terileptils aren't far away. Unlike many alien monsters, you can shoot or burn a Terileptil, so you have some chance of winning a fight.

MONSTER DATA

ORIGIN

Terileptus

SIZE

SPEED

SLOW — FAST

0 1 2 3 4 5 6 7 8 9 10

DANGEROUS RATING

SAFE — DEADLY

0 1 2 3 4 5 6 7 8 9 10

TIME BEETLE

THE TIME BEETLE IS ONE OF THE TRICKSTER'S BRIGADE.
It feeds on the what-ifs and the might-have-beens every time
you make a choice. One changed Donna's choices so that she
never met me - and that had terrible consequences . . .

Once it latches on to
your back, a Time Beetle
can change your life.

I mean that - it can
change what's happened
to you in the past.

SURVIVAL TIPS

You probably won't even
realise events are changing.
But, if you can tell there's
something wrong, then you
have to get time back on
track somehow. Not easy -
even for me. Good luck!

Try as you might, you won't be able to
see it without special tech.

MONSTER DATA

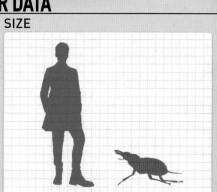

ORIGIN

One of the Trickster's Brigade

SIZE

SPEED

SLOW | | | | | | | | | | FAST
0 1 2 3 4 (5) 6 7 8 9 (10)

DANGEROUS RATING

SAFE | | | | | | | | | | DEADLY
0 1 2 3 4 (5) 6 7 8 9 (10)

PYROVILE

A RACE COMPOSED OF ROCK AND FIRE. A group of Pyroviles hid in Mount Vesuvius, near Pompeii. They planned to boil away the seas and oceans, then weld themselves to humans, creating a new species. Not a terrifically friendly or sensible plan.

Ability to incinerate victims in seconds.

Crusty, rocky skin.

Internal fire keeps rock in a molten state.

SURVIVAL TIPS

Even if you don't see them, breathing in Pyrovile dust particles can turn you into living rock. How to destroy them? Not easy. But if there's an active volcano handy, set it off and they'll cause you no more trouble.

MONSTER DATA

ORIGIN

Pyrovillia

SPEED

SLOW									FAST
0	1	2	3	4	5	6	7	8	9	10

DANGEROUS RATING

SAFE									DEADLY
0	1	2	3	4	5	6	7	8	9	10

SIZE

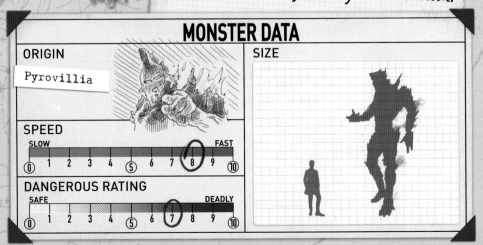

THE FLOOD

WATER GETS EVERYWHERE. It always
finds a way - through the ground or
between the cracks. The Flood lives
in water. It infected the water on
Mars, and you only have to touch
it for it to infect you too -
it'll turn you into a mutated
creature with cracked skin
and constantly dripping with
water. Just a single drop
will do it.

Cracked skin.

Ability to shoot infected
water from hands and mouth.

Just one drop will do this to you.
Remember that. One drop.

I ran into the Flood on Bowie Base One on Mars. It infected the crew, and planned to travel back to Earth and infect everyone there. I managed to save some of the people and get them home before the base was destroyed. But, if they brought just one drop of water back with them . . .

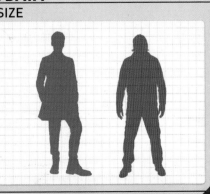

MONSTER DATA

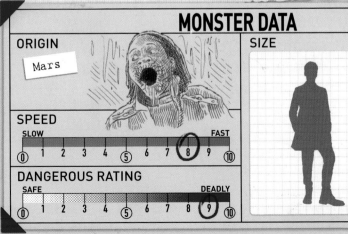

ORIGIN

Mars

SPEED

SLOW — FAST
0 1 2 3 4 5 6 7 8 9 10

DANGEROUS RATING

SAFE — DEADLY
0 1 2 3 4 5 6 7 8 9 10

SIZE

THE ICE WARRIORS

AN ANCIENT AND NOBLE RACE, THE
ORIGINAL INHABITANTS OF MARS
WERE NICKNAMED ICE WARRIORS
BECAUSE THEY LIKE THE COLD.
Can't stand heat, in fact. They
look like big green reptile-
men, but most of what
you can see is their
armour. War is like
an art form to them -
'Death or Glory' is
an Ice Warrior motto.
Says it all, really.

Ice Warriors
like the cold.

Scaly shell is
actually armour.

Weapons kill with sonic technology.

Big, strong, dangerous.

142

In the future, the Ice Warriors are less hostile and actually join the Galactic Federation. I was on the planet Peladon when it decided to join, too. And again, fifty years later, when a group of rogue Ice Warriors tried to take it over - so they hadn't all completely changed.

MONSTER DATA

ORIGIN

Mars

SIZE

SPEED

SLOW   FAST

0   1   2   3   4   **(5)**   6   7   8   9   10

DANGEROUS RATING

SAFE   DEADLY

0   1   2   3   4   5   6   7   **(8)**   9   10

THE SILURIANS

IT'S ALL A MISUNDERSTANDING REALLY. The Silurians were on Earth millions of years ago, but went into hibernation. When they woke up they still thought, not surprisingly, that Earth was their planet. They see you and me - well, you, anyway - as sort of upstart monkeys. So they'd like to get rid of you and have their planet back.

There are several types of Silurian.

They're not from the Silurian era at all.

That's just what someone who found them thought.

Claws, teeth, and a vicious poisonous tongue.

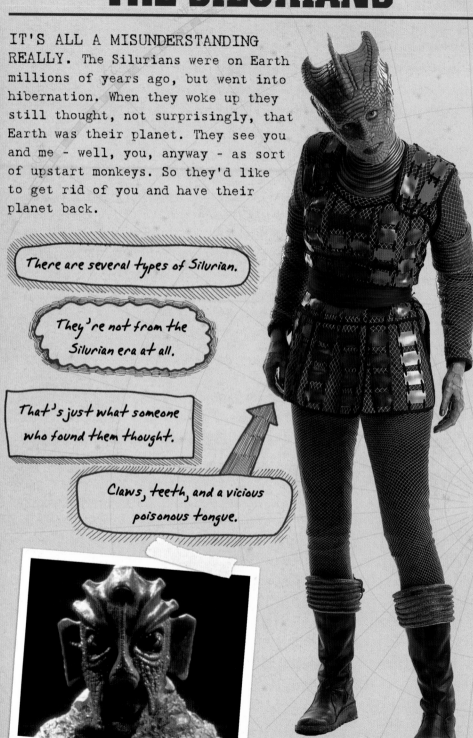

The Silurians went into hibernation because a small planet was approaching through space, and they thought it would hit Earth. But it didn't. The catastrophe never happened, and the Silurians didn't wake up. The small planet got caught by Earth's gravity and became the moon . . .

SURVIVAL TIPS

Lots of things that can wake Silurians – drilling, mining, anything that disturbs the ground near a hibernation centre. If they do wake, try to explain that you can share the planet. If that fails, see if you can put them back to sleep. Not by singing a lullaby – that's unlikely to work.

MONSTER DATA

ORIGIN

Prehistoric Earth

SIZE

SPEED

SLOW – FAST: 0 1 2 3 4 5 6 7 8 9 10 (7 circled)

DANGEROUS RATING

SAFE – DEADLY: 0 1 2 3 4 5 6 7 8 9 10 (7 circled)

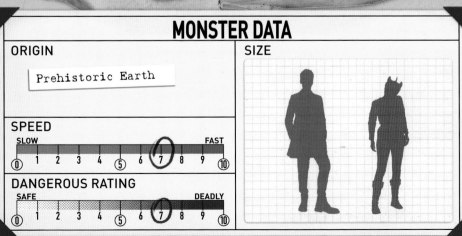

THE SEA DEVILS

UNDERWATER SILURIANS - THEY WERE CALLED SEA DEVILS BY THE POOR CHAP WHO ACCIDENTALLY WOKE THEM WHILE REPAIRING AN OLD SEA FORT. Not only that, but the Master was in prison on an island nearby; it didn't take him long to get involved and persuade the Sea Devils to get rid of humanity and take back their planet.

An aquatic type of Silurian.

Hand-held heat-ray gun. *

Not sure about the blue string vest, to be honest.

Double trouble when Silurians and Sea Devils both attacked Sea Base 4 and tried to start a nuclear war to destroy all human life. They had a Myrka too - that's a sort of small dinosaur with electrified skin. Touch it, and ZAPP! So don't touch it. Obviously.

SURVIVAL TIPS

Like with the Silurians, if you can sit down and have a sensible little talk - maybe with tea and biscuits - then you might resolve things. Having the Master stirring things up didn't help when I tried . . . so the Royal Navy blew up the Sea Devils' base. Rather extreme, but I have to admit it worked.

MONSTER DATA

ORIGIN

Prehistoric Earth

SIZE

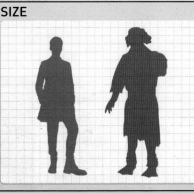

SPEED

SLOW — FAST
0 1 2 3 4 5 6 (7) 8 9 10

DANGEROUS RATING

SAFE — DEADLY
0 1 2 3 4 5 6 (7) 8 9 10

DINOSAURS

WELL, WHO DOESN'T KNOW WHAT DINOSAURS ARE? COME ON - OF COURSE YOU DO. You'll also know they all died out millions of years ago . . . except the ones that left Earth with some escaping Silurians. And the dinosaurs that Professor Whitaker brought to modern London with a time scoop. You might think something's extinct but, with time travel, you can never be sure.

It's a dinosaur.

With me riding on it.

Not usually a good move, though.

Luckily, this is a Triceratops, and they only eat plants.

I arrived in London once to find it deserted except for the army and a load of dinosaurs. A group of idealists had brought dinosaurs through time in order to clear London, return the world to prehistoric times and start history all over again. Like they'd do any better than last time.

MONSTER DATA

ORIGIN

Prehistoric Earth

SPEED

SLOW

Varies depending on species

① 1 2 3 4 ⑤ 6 7 8 9 ⑩

DANGEROUS RATING

SAFE   DEADLY

Varies depending on species

SIZE

SOLOMON'S ROBOTS

ROBOTS ARE ONLY AS GOOD - OR AS BAD - AS WHOEVER CONTROLS THEM. So the two robots that Solomon had on his stolen Silurian Ark were pretty bad. Solomon got them to eject the Silurians into space so he could have their dinosaurs.

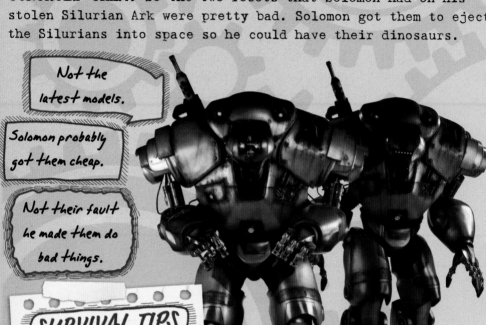

Not the latest models.

Solomon probably got them cheap.

Not their fault he made them do bad things.

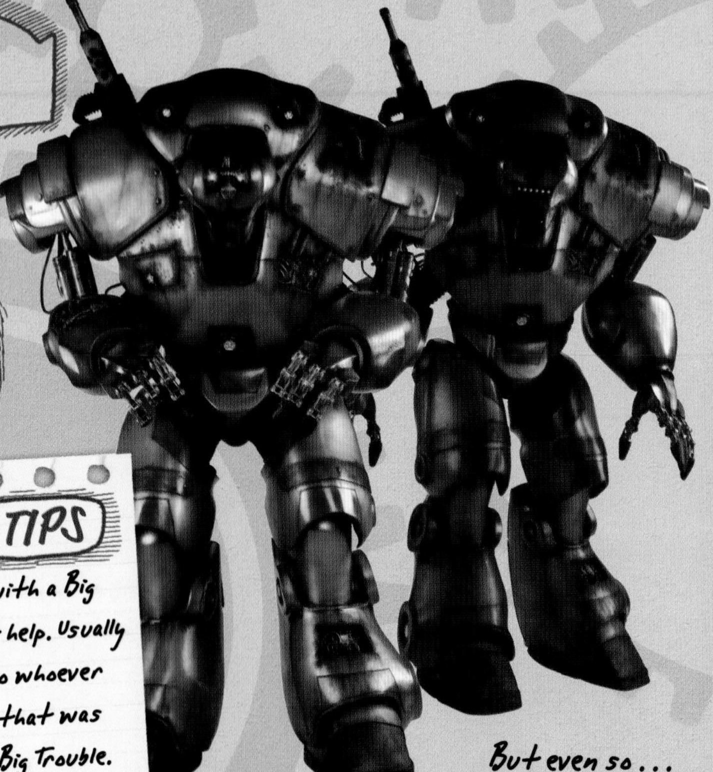

SURVIVAL TIPS

Arguing the point with a Big Robot probably won't help. Usually you'll need to get to whoever controls them. If that was Solomon you'd be in Big Trouble.

But even so...

MONSTER DATA

ORIGIN

Belonged to Solomon

- not a nice man

SPEED

SLOW — FAST: 0 1 2 3 4 5 6 7 8 9 10 (4 circled)

DANGEROUS RATING

SAFE — DEADLY: 0 1 2 3 4 5 6 7 8 9 10 (6 circled)

SIZE

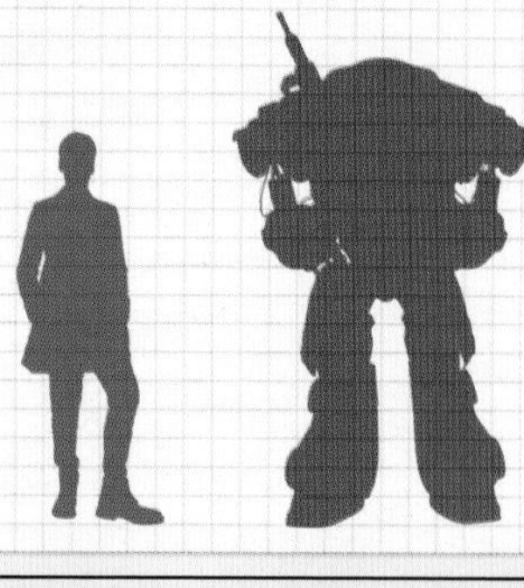

HOUSE

WHAT A STUPID NAME. I mean, he wasn't a house - he was a disembodied mind living inside an asteroid in a bubble universe separate from our own. He fed on TARDISes. He tried to eat mine. But we stopped him, my TARDIS and me.

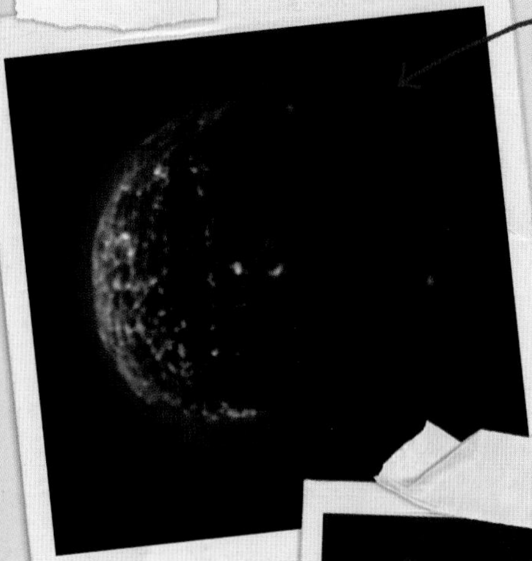

House fed on artron energy.

He lured many other Time Lords to their doom.

The eleven-dimensional personality matrix of my TARDIS got put into a mad, bitey woman called Idris.

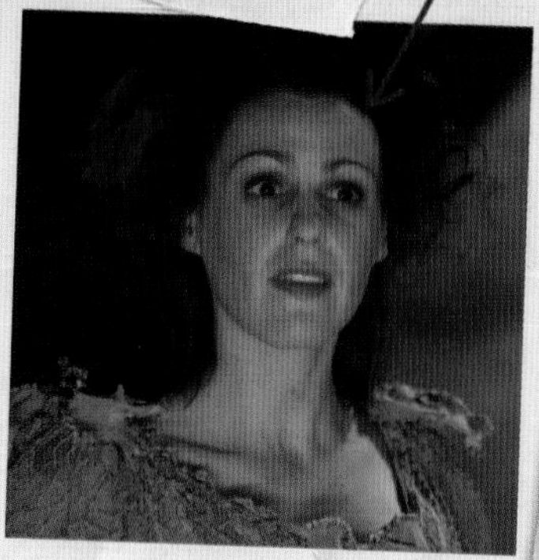

My TARDIS became a person! Bit of a shock.

SURVIVAL TIPS

Not a lot you can do if your TARDIS is caught by House, apart from staying away from asteroids in bubble universes. Your greatest ally will be your own TARDIS. Your greatest friend, too...

MONSTER DATA

ORIGIN

A bubble universe

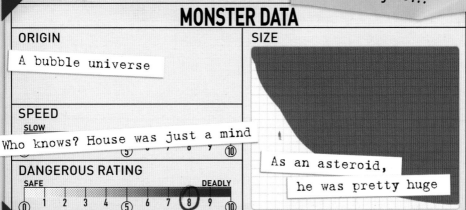

SPEED

SLOW

Who knows? House was just a mind

DANGEROUS RATING

SAFE — DEADLY

0 1 2 3 4 5 6 7 (8) 9 10

SIZE

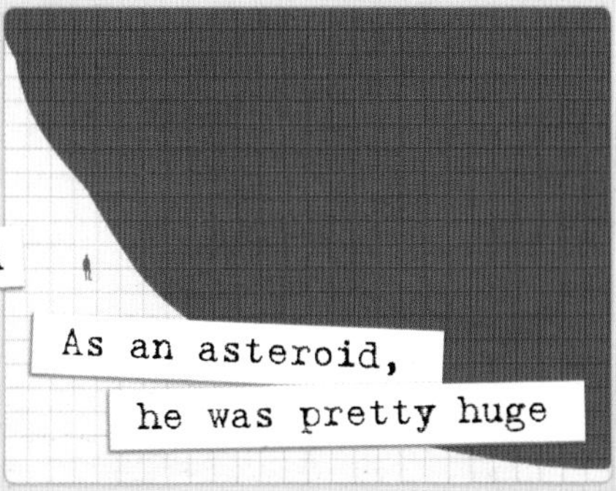

As an asteroid, he was pretty huge

THE SHAKRI

THE SHAKRI THINK OF THEMSELVES AS THE PEST CONTROLLERS OF THE UNIVERSE. They follow the Tally, also known as Judgement Day or the Reckoning. It's all a bit confusing, to be honest. But, basically, the Shakri see humanity as a contagion that needs to be wiped out. They look pretty human themselves - well, not pretty pretty. More sort of wizened and wrinkled.

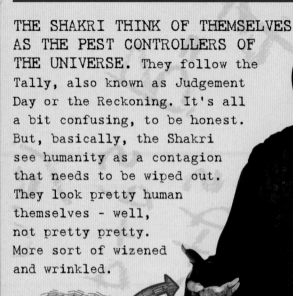

Seriously long talons.

This one was actually a hologram.

They see humans as a contagion to be eradicated.

As well as sending loads of cubes to Earth to assess humanity and find its weaknesses, the Shakri also used an android to oversee the operation. She looked just like a little girl except her eyes glowed blue, which was a bit of a giveaway. My sonic screwdriver sorted her out.

SURVIVAL TIPS

Cubes: that's what the Shakri use. Remember the Slow Invasion? I thought not – human memories are so unreliable. But, if loads of black cubes appear all over the world (again), beware! They're testing people, looking for weak points, preparing to attack. Gather them all together and blow them up!

MONSTER DATA

ORIGIN | The Shakri claim to live in 'all of time and none' - whatever that means

SIZE

SPEED

SLOW ——————————— FAST
0 1 2 3 4 ⑤ 6 7 8 9 10

DANGEROUS RATING

SAFE ——————————— DEADLY
0 1 2 3 4 ⑤ 6 ⑦ 8 9 10

PRISONER ZERO

WELL, HE WAS SUPPOSED TO BE A PRISONER, HELD IN AN EXTRA-DIMENSIONAL PRISON BY THE ATRAXI. But he escaped through a crack in time into Amy Pond's bedroom. He hid in her house for twelve years without anyone noticing. Twelve years! How long does it take to spot a gelatinous snake creature that can shape-shift into anything it's formed a psychic link with?

Multi-form shape-shifting alien.

Looks like a big snake with loads of teeth.

But he can shape-shift into other forms.

I've no idea what the Atraxi look like. But their spaceships are like huge crystalline eyeballs. No face - just the eye with spikes coming off it. They tracked Prisoner Zero to Earth after he escaped, and would have destroyed the whole world just to get their prisoner back.

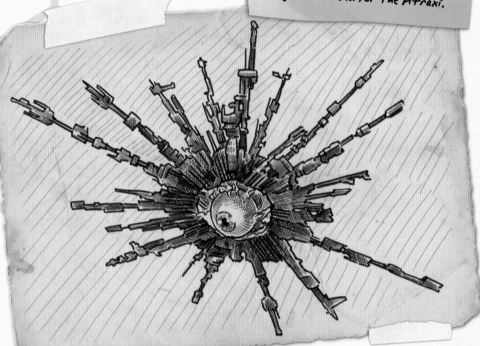

MONSTER DATA

ORIGIN

Unknown

SPEED

SLOW · 0 · 1 · 2 · 3 · 4 · 5 · 6 · 7 · 8 · 9 · 10 · FAST

DANGEROUS RATING

SAFE · 0 · 1 · 2 · 3 · 4 · 5 · 6 · 7 · 8 · 9 · 10 · DEADLY

SIZE

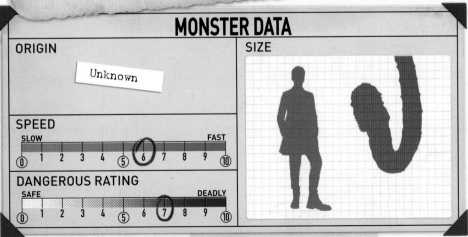

SILENTS

THEY'RE ACTUALLY PRIESTS - NOT THAT YOU'D GUESS. The Silents are tall, pale, gaunt creatures in skinny suits. As soon as you look away from them, you forget them. They were here on Earth for a long time, influencing human development. And no one noticed. Or rather, no one remembered. Sorry, what was I saying?

This is what a Silent looks like.

Though you'll forget that as soon as you turn the page.

Shoots electricity from its fingers.

A breakaway group of Silents worked with Madame Kovarian and her allies to try to get me killed by the Ponds' daughter, River Song. All so I'd never go to Trenzalore. They were afraid I'd bring Gallifrey back into this universe, and the Time Lords would reappear.

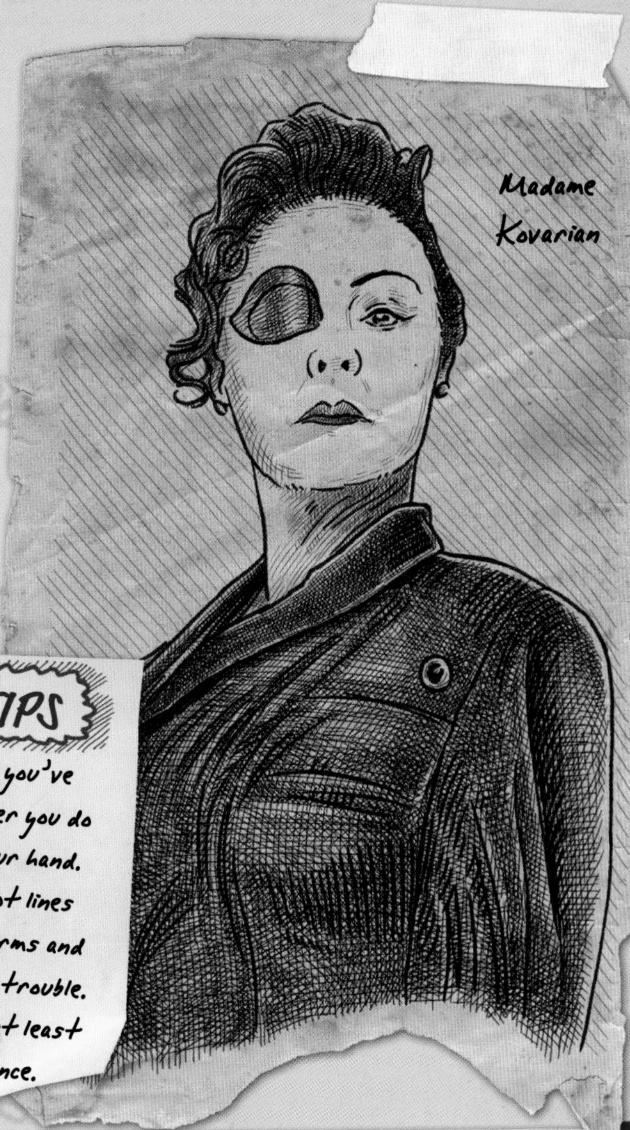

SURVIVAL TIPS

You won't remember if you've seen a Silent. So, whenever you do see one, draw a line on your hand. Then if you find you've got lines all over your hands (and arms and face) you'll know you're in trouble. Not much you can do, but at least you won't die in ignorance.

MONSTER DATA

ORIGIN Confessional Priests of the Church of the Silence - formerly the Papal Mainframe

SPEED

SLOW 0 1 2 3 4 5 (6) 7 8 9 10 FAST

DANGEROUS RATING

SAFE 0 1 2 3 4 5 6 7 (8) 9 10 DEADLY

SIZE

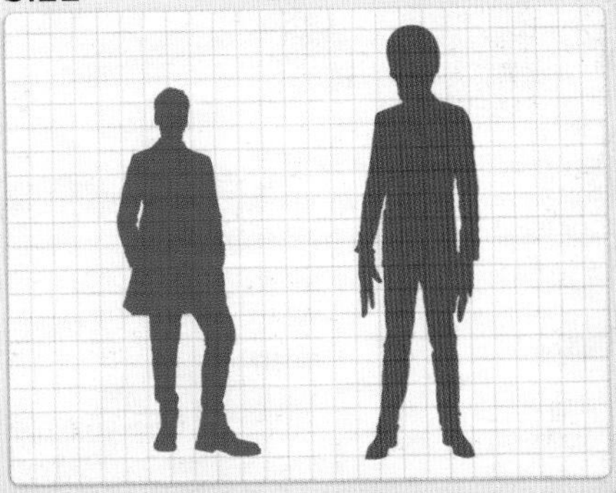

THE SIREN

IN MYTHOLOGY, THE SIRENS WERE
WOMEN WHOSE SINGING LURED
SAILORS TO CRASH ON THE
ROCKS. The Siren I met
on board the pirate ship
Fancy was an alien
hologram that
appeared through
a temporal
rift from any
reflective
surface - like
metal or glass or
water. And there
was a lot of calm
water about.
She made people
disappear, but
actually she was
trying to help them.

She's actually a
virtual doctor
from another
dimension.

Her song anaesthetises
people, putting their
bodies in stasis.

She hates germs and
will sterilise with fire,
so watch out!

Captain Henry Avery, notorious pirate. Good mate of mine, once I'd saved him from the Siren. Although then he was stuck on a Skerth ship, with a crew that would die if they left. The Siren was a medical interface that 'repaired' the crew when they got injured - but the repairs only worked on the Skerth ship.

SURVIVAL TIPS

The problem with the Siren was that she had no sense of proportion. Just a small cut, and she thought you needed mending. She'd take you off to the Skerth ship and fix you - which is all fine and dandy, except you can never leave. So don't get injured on a pirate ship.

MONSTER DATA

ORIGIN

Came through a temporal rift from a Skerth ship in another dimension

SPEED

SLOW — FAST
0 1 2 3 4 (5) 6 7 ⑧ 9 10

DANGEROUS RATING

SAFE — DEADLY
0 1 2 3 4 (5) ⑥ 7 8 9 10

SIZE

SIL

UNPLEASANT, GREEN, SLOBBERING GIANT SLUG THING.
That's about it really. He was one of the Mentors, and they'll do anything for profit. Sil would sell his own grandmother if there were money in it, so he'd certainly sell (or kill) you . . .

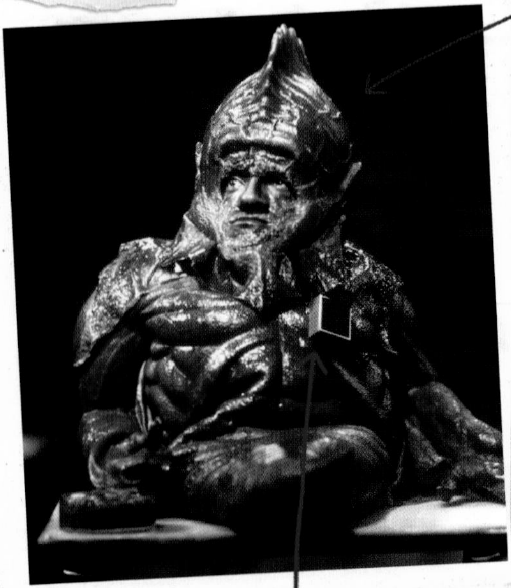

Slimy and yucky.

Sil likes eating marsh minnows.

Needs constant moisturising in a dry climate.

Rubbish voice translator that keeps getting it wrong.

SURVIVAL TIPS

You'll know when Sil is around. You'll probably hear him laughing – a globby, slobbery sound. Don't let him think you're valuable. Offer him a marsh minnow. Or crash the financial markets – that'll distract him.

MONSTER DATA

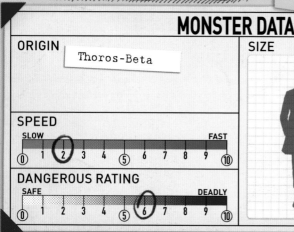

ORIGIN

Thoros-Beta

SIZE

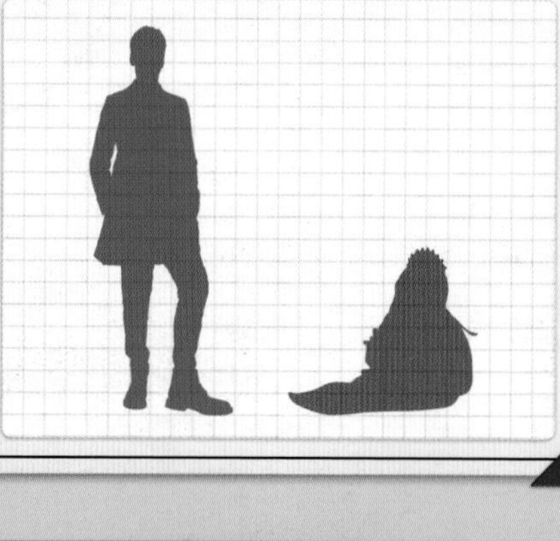

SPEED

SLOW — FAST

0 1 [2] 3 4 5 6 7 8 9 10

DANGEROUS RATING

SAFE — DEADLY

0 1 2 3 4 5 [6] 7 8 9 10

HEADLESS MONKS

MONKS, WITH NO HEADS. What more do you need to know? Under their hoods - no heads. That's it. They had some notion that faith comes from the heart, and the head is full of doubt. Or something. Seems crazy to me.

Looks like an ordinary monk.

But under the hood - nothing. No head. Hence 'headless'.

SURVIVAL TIPS

You'd think monks would be quiet and peaceful. Not this lot. If you spot a suspiciously short monk with his hood up and no face, keep well back before he whips out his power sword and comes after your head.

Vicious with a sword.

MONSTER DATA

ORIGIN Overseen by the Papal Mainframe, their last resting place was the Delirium Archive

SIZE

SPEED

SLOW — FAST
0 1 2 3 4 (5) 6 7 8 9 10

DANGEROUS RATING

SAFE — DEADLY
0 1 2 3 4 (5) 6 (7) 8 9 10

TESELECTA

A MACHINE THAT CAN TRAVEL THROUGH TIME AND SPACE
AND CHANGE ITS SHAPE. No, not the TARDIS - if it worked.
The Teselecta was a Justice Department vehicle that changed
its appearance to look like people. And it wasn't bigger on
the inside; the crew got smaller to fit. The crew hunted down
criminals - including River Song - through time and space and
punished them with death. Not a good move.

Crew is kept miniaturised by a compression field.

It can adapt itself
to look like anyone or
anything it has scanned.

Anyone inside who isn't authorised to be
on board is eliminated by robot antibodies.

You don't want to get on the wrong side of a Teselecta. Or on the inside, if you're not invited - as its antibodies will get you. But a Teselecta helped me at Lake Silencio. The Teselecta took my form so that, when spacesuited River shot it, everyone thought it was me who was dead. Brilliant.

SURVIVAL TIPS

The Teselecta looks – and behaves – just like a real person. Maybe even someone you know. Maybe even a friend (if you have one). But the good news is it's only after criminals. So behave yourself and you should be OK.

MONSTER DATA

ORIGIN

The Justice Department

SPEED

SLOW 0 1 2 3 4 5 6 (7) 8 9 10 FAST

DANGEROUS RATING

SAFE 0 1 2 3 4 5 6 (7) 8 9 10 DEADLY

SIZE

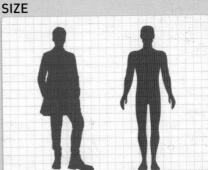

PEG DOLLS

I ONCE GOT SHRUNK DOWN AND STUCK INSIDE A DOLL'S HOUSE. And the dolls - human-sized peg dolls made from old-fashioned clothes pegs - were alive. Not only that, if they caught you, they'd turn you into wooden dolls, too.

Big dolls. Or, rather, small people.

They were led by a dancer doll and a soldier doll.

SURVIVAL TIPS

Don't upset a Tenza child. They hatch in the millions, and then find suitable foster families. The child becomes one of the family ... unless it feels insecure. Then bad things happen. So be nice to kids, OK?

They sang me a rhyme about clocks. I didn't like it.

MONSTER DATA

ORIGIN

Brought to life by George, a Tenza child

SIZE

SPEED

SLOW   FAST
0 1 2 3 4 (5) 6 7 8 9 (10)

DANGEROUS RATING

SAFE   DEADLY
0 1 2 3 4 (5) 6 7 8 9 (10)

THE TERRIBLE ZODIN

SHE WAS CALLED TERRIBLE BECAUSE SHE WAS. Ugly creature with claws, she got up to all sorts of mischief. Helped by giant grasshoppers. Or was it mutant kangaroos? Maybe it was both. I've run into her a few times . . .

Clawed hands.

Hooked nose.

The fact she looks rather like a witch is a hint.

Not to be confused with the race of Zodin – they are friendly, and look like Fimbles.

SURVIVAL TIPS

Watch out for those giant grasshoppers and mutant kangaroos. They should be easy to spot – even for you. If you do meet Zodin, tweak her nose. She hates that.

MONSTER DATA

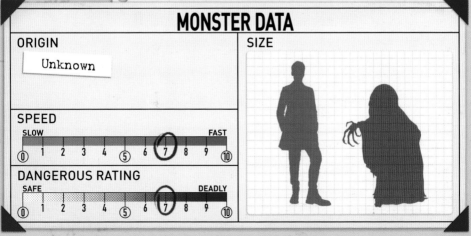

ORIGIN

Unknown

SPEED

SLOW   FAST
0 1 2 3 4 5 6 7 8 9 10

DANGEROUS RATING

SAFE   DEADLY
0 1 2 3 4 5 6 7 8 9 10

SIZE

GANGERS

SHORT FOR 'DOPPELGANGERS', WHICH JUST MEANS 'DOUBLES', REALLY. The Gangers were copies of people made from a substance called the Flesh. It wasn't real flesh, but a synthetic replica. The Gangers were expendable - if they died, the real people they were copied from lived on, no problem. But some of the Gangers didn't think that was altogether fair. So - rebellion!

Gangers look just like the real people.

Features can blur and dissolve.

They have the memories and personality of the original person.

Eyes and minds form first.

I was taken in by a Ganger once. Actually, I was a Ganger once, but that was planned. Not so planned, however, was Amy being replaced by a Ganger - she just dissolved into a puddle of white goo. Then, when we got her back, her baby Melody was also replaced. Should have spotted that coming really.

SURVIVAL TIPS

Most Gangers are happy with their lot, and resigned to their (probably) short lives. But they can go rogue. Watch out for faces that get blurred like they're actually made from a thick, sticky liquid rather than real skin and bone. Because, if they do blur, then maybe they are rogue.

MONSTER DATA

ORIGIN

Created from Flesh by the Morpeth-Jetsan company

SPEED

SLOW — FAST

0 1 2 3 4 5 6 7 8 9 10 (7 circled)

DANGEROUS RATING

SAFE — DEADLY

0 1 2 3 4 5 6 7 8 9 10 (8 circled)

SIZE

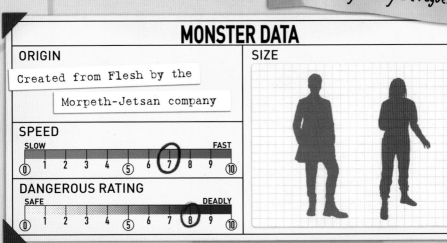

THE GUNSLINGER

KAHLER-TEK WAS A HUMAN CYBORG - PART PERSON, PART WAR MACHINE, DESIGNED TO KILL. But he got damaged so that when the war was over he didn't deactivate. Instead, he hunted down the scientists who had turned him into a killing machine. He found the last one, Kahler-Jex, in a town called Mercy in the Wild West.

Robot eye.

Used to be human.

Now, not so much.

Energy weapon built into arm.

Bent on revenge.

Kahler-Jex hid in a town called Mercy, doing his best to help out - by installing electric lights before they'd actually been invented, for example. Tut tut. But it couldn't make up for what he'd done to Kahler-Tek and the other cyborgs. I think Jex knew that, deep down. I guess we're all guilty of something . . .

MONSTER DATA

ORIGIN

Gabrean on the planet Kahler

SPEED

SLOW ⸺⸺⸺⸺⸺⸺⸺⸺ FAST
⓪ 1 2 3 4 ⑤ ⑥ 7 8 9 ⑩

DANGEROUS RATING

SAFE ⸺⸺⸺⸺⸺⸺⸺⸺ DEADLY
⓪ 1 2 3 4 ⑤ 6 7 8 ⑨ ⑩

SIZE

THE GREAT INTELLIGENCE

WELL, IT CERTAINLY WASN'T MODEST, WAS IT? I MEAN, CALLING ITSELF THE GREAT INTELLIGENCE. But then that was all it was: just a mind without a body. Until it found something to give it life. It took over so many people, but perhaps the most dangerous was Doctor Walter Simeon - the Intelligence took him over when he was just a child.

> The Great Intelligence 'possessed' a snowman it'd made, channelling all its dark thoughts into the snowman.

It must have seemed like it had given the snowman life.

It had the power to freeze victims by touching them.

Without its own body, the Great Intelligence either steals other people's bodies or animates objects. It created a copy of the Latimer family's governess out of ice from the pond in which she drowned. Being confronted by a governess is scary enough - but a dead one made of ice?

SURVIVAL TIPS

The Great Intelligence really doesn't like me. It even tried to erase my entire existence. A bit extreme, but the Great Intelligence is like that. It'll kill anyone who gets in its way. So don't get in its way. If you do, try to find out who the Great Intelligence is controlling and break the connection.

MONSTER DATA

ORIGIN Unknown

SPEED Unknown

SLOW 0 1 2 3 4 5 6 7 8 9 10 FAST

DANGEROUS RATING

SAFE 0 1 2 3 4 5 6 7 8 9 10 DEADLY (9 circled)

SIZE

SNOWMEN

THE GREAT INTELLIGENCE CREATED A SWARM OF LIVING SNOW - MULTI-NUCLEATE CRYSTAL ORGANISMS WHICH GENERATED A LOW TELEPATHIC FIELD. Doesn't matter if you don't understand that, so long as you know what it means - and it means vicious, killer snowmen that eat humans.

It's a snowman.

With teeth.

And, yes, given the chance it will eat you.

SURVIVAL TIPS

If you see a snowman that looks hungry, do your best to melt it using your mind. If that fails, you can hose it away with warm water, use salt to raise the freezing point or just hope the weather improves.

MONSTER DATA

ORIGIN

Created from real snow but given life by the Great Intelligence

SPEED

SLOW 0 1 2 3 4 **5** 6 7 8 9 10 FAST

DANGEROUS RATING

SAFE 0 1 2 3 4 5 6 7 **8** 9 10 DEADLY

SIZE

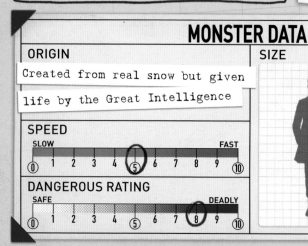

THE YETI

THE YETI - OR ABOMINABLE SNOWMEN - I MET WERE ROBOTS. The Great Intelligence used them to try to take over a monastery in Tibet, and then the world. After I stopped it, the Great Intelligence tried again, sending Yeti into the London Underground.

Looks like a real Abominable Snowman.

But it's a robot.

Controlled by the Great Intelligence.

Strong, savage and dangerous!

SURVIVAL TIPS

Too strong for you to fight, and bullets have no effect. But, if you can get the control sphere out of its chest, the Yeti is just a heap of metal and fur.

MONSTER DATA

ORIGIN

Robots created by the Great Intelligence

SPEED

SLOW — FAST

0 1 2 3 4 5 6 7 8 9 10

DANGEROUS RATING

SAFE — DEADLY

0 1 2 3 4 5 6 7 8 9 10

SIZE

THE WHISPER MEN

DO YOU KNOW THE RHYME?

Do you hear the Whisper Men? The Whisper Men are near.

If you hear the Whisper Men, then turn away your ear.

Do not hear the Whisper Men, whatever else you do.

For once you've heard the Whisper Men, they'll stop and look at you.

The Whisper Men, created by the
Great Intelligence, are not real.
But they can really kill you.

Looks like they're hollow
inside. Maybe they are.

Vicious teeth.

They appear — and
disappear — at the
speed of thought.

If the Whisper Men talk, it'll probably be in rhyme. Don't know why, but it's annoying. Here's my rhyme for you:

Do you hear the Whisper Men, are they on their way?

If you see the Whisper Men, then turn and run away.

SURVIVAL TIPS

Remember how I said not to get in the way of the Great Intelligence? The Whisper Men are another good reason for that. They just appear, whenever and wherever the Great Intelligence wants, and they can reach inside you and stop your heart. And you don't want that.

MONSTER DATA

ORIGIN	SIZE

Created by the Great Intelligence

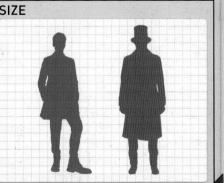

SPEED

SLOW ⓪ 1 2 3 4 ⑤ 6 7 ⑧ 9 ⑩ FAST

DANGEROUS RATING

SAFE ⓪ 1 2 3 4 ⑤ 6 7 ⑧ 9 ⑩ DEADLY

THE FINAL WORD

NO, THE FINAL WORD
ISN'T A HORRIFIC AND
TERRIFYING MONSTER.

It's me. Again.

Giving some advice. Again.

So pay attention this time.

After all, it's your life

I'm trying to save.

We've been through a lot
of dangerous monsters in this book - some more
dangerous than others. But, whatever the monster, and
however dangerous it is, there are a few basic rules.

1. DO AS I SAY. ALWAYS. NO QUESTIONS. BECAUSE I'M RIGHT AND YOU'RE PROBABLY WRONG.

2. TRUST YOUR INSTINCTS. IF YOU THINK YOU MIGHT BE IN TROUBLE, YOU PROBABLY ARE. IF YOU KNOW YOU'RE IN TROUBLE, THEN YOU'RE IN BIG TROUBLE.

3. KEEP ALERT. WATCH OUT. LISTEN HARD. BE ON YOUR GUARD.

4. IF IN DOUBT, HIDE. NOT UNDER THE BED, BECAUSE A MONSTER MIGHT HAVE BEATEN YOU TO IT. BUT BEHIND THE SOFA IS GOOD.

5. FAILING THAT: RUN!